MADISON ROSIPAL

The Forsaken Prince

This book is dedicated to my amazing family and friends who have supported me since day one. Especially to my parents and grandparents, who love me unconditionally, and gave me the confidence to write.
Thank you also for my fantastic Beta Readers, whose kind feedback spurred me forward. Especially Arion M, D, Ezra (EMP), Kim Folkestad, Ziggy, Nicole B, Kim P, Adair Orion, Chen Puchailo, and the others who chose not to be named.

Chapter 1

Dawn was just beginning to break when Princess Celestine of Yulia awoke. She had an early start, with a long list of duties for the day. Her morning routine rarely took much time, as she had grown accustomed to having to get ready in a hurry. A quick brush of her wavy brown hair, a well-thought-out outfit, and a freshly brushed smile was all she needed to look her best. After a quick check to make sure her pantsuit was perfectly neat, she stepped out of her room and into the hall.

Walking toward her first destination, she ran through her checklist in her head. The stone walls of the castle seemed to melt away into static with how laser-focused she was on her duties. Celestine had a collection of attributes that were working against her, so to make up for that, she worked twice as hard.

The kingdom of Yulia, one of the most ancient on the continent of Abela has, for centuries, stood as an icon of order and justice. Economically, Yulia was one of the major powerhouses of the West and had been for centuries. There was a massive range of fertile land that the kingdom took advantage of, as well as several families of talented smiths who contributed to the production of military supplies for the entire world. Yet, it was their hatred of magic and those who wielded it that was most infamous. They weren't the only ones who participated in the slaughter, but they were the most notorious.

She learned about it in her history studies, how her ancestors massacred magic users and criminalized its practice: serving as judge, jury, and executioner for an entire group of people. Since the magic community took up only a small portion of the population at that point, it made it impossible for them to fight back. They scattered, settling in kingdoms that accepted them or establishing their own.

As time went on, Yulian leaders were strategic. They made sure they only killed those within their boarders, and focused most of their trade with nations that agreed with their beliefs. To maintain the peace, they were civil with magic nations that they deemed "virtuous", but they didn't like it. Were it not for the threat of war, they would have massacred without limit.

It was horrid to imagine, but thankfully, after almost 400 years, these practices were abolished over a century ago by King Titus. The kingdom had become more accepting, so it was mostly a formality. Unfortunately for her, however, she was the first royal since to be born with the gift of magic. This "gift" ostracized her from the rest of her family and brought unwanted attention from from the tiny pockets of society that once deemed her kind criminal. She decided at a young age to rise above all this and become the most incredible magician Queen they had ever seen.

She studied day in and day out to be a good queen, so she could create a world where she and others like her could live in pure peace. If she wasn't sleeping, bathing, or eating, she had her face buried in a book or was listening to a lecture. This was great for her academic career, but not for her social life. In her 17 years of life, she hadn't made any friends outside of her family.

"Good morning, Princess," A young maid who she believed was new, said to her as she passed.

"Good morning," She replied robotically, mind elsewhere.

Before she could get started with work, she had to stop by the dining room for breakfast. Can't run on an empty stomach after all. Her mother and father, Queen Eileena and King Jacob, were already waiting for her by the time she got there. That was to be expected, the king and queen always had more chores than anyone else and had to get up earlier to accommodate.

Her father looked up from his paperwork when she walked in, his trademark royal purple eyes meeting her own. The queen was busy talking to one of the chefs and hadn't noticed her daughter yet.

"Good morning, darling," Her father called, waving for her to join.

"Good morning, father," She replied with a formal bow.

The dining room was massive, with room for well over twenty people at a time, perfect for political dinners and grand banquets, but for day-to-day purposes, there were only four chairs. Her father's chair sat at the head of the table, with her mother's to his right, Celestine's to his left, and her brother's beside the queen's. They tried to eat all of their meals together, whenever work would allow, but today it seemed that her brother, Prince Hesperus, had gotten a head start, as his place was empty.

As Celestine pulled out her chair, her mother acknowledged

her with a smile. Her emerald green eyes shined with love.

The royal family has, for as long as history could recall, always had purple eyes. According to history, an ancient king was shown the true way to lead a kingdom by god, and was thus marked with purple eyes. Every single child born to a member of the royal family had purple eyes after that. More than likely, it was just a combination of a mutation coupled with strong genetics, but they preferred the "blessed by god" story.

They varied in shade from person to person, but they were always some variation of purple. Celestine's father's were on the grayer side of violet, while hers were electric purple, and her brother's were a bright lilac, identical to the color's namesake. They were the direct descendants of the family, while her mother had married in, marked by her emerald green eyes.

"Your brother left us early to get a head start on training. Poor thing is going to make himself sick," Her mother explained, gesturing to the empty chair.

Celestine raised her hands to allow a maid to place a perfectly pressed napkin in her lap before speaking.

"He sure is determined. It's good to see him so passionate about something."

"I agree. It's good for him," Her father added.

The maid returned with a plate of Celestine's favorite breakfast, a stack of pancakes with a variety of fruits and toppings. Syrup trickled beautifully down the sides, carrying speckles of powdered sugar. It made her mouth water every time.

As she tucked into her breakfast, her father stood, setting down the cup of coffee he'd been nursing.

"Pardon me, ladies, but I've a hearing to preside over in a few minutes," He explained.

Chapter 1

Leaving the mess he made, he walked to his wife and placed a sweet goodbye kiss on her lips. Celestine received one on the cheek as he walked past, as well as a loving, fatherly pat on the head.

The two ladies continued eating in silence. It wasn't the poignant silence that often exists between mother and daughter, rather, it was the silence created when two people are hungry and working through their meal. When her mother finished her bowl of porridge, she daintily wiped her mouth.

"How have your studies been going as of late? Was that book of any use to you?" She began.

"They've been well, the grimoire has certainly been interesting, but I haven't managed to make any major progress."

The queen had always been supportive of her daughter's endeavors with magic. Her side of the family came from the region of the kingdom that opposed the harsh oppression of magic, meaning she was much more open-minded about it. It never impacted her directly, but as a child, the queen had seen the few magic users her region had helping the community, so the harsh whispers of the past never reached her ears.

A few weeks prior, while on a diplomatic trip, the queen was gifted a beautiful grimoire that was written in one of the surrounding kingdoms. She was told it was a very exquisite and rare volume, one magicians of all walks of life coveted. Immediately, her first thought was to give it to her daughter in the hopes that it could teach her what she couldn't.

Even with all the work the royal family had been doing in the years after magic was decriminalized, there was still only a tiny population of magic users, and there were no reputable instructors among them, so Celestine had been on her own until that point. This was the first book on magic she'd been exposed to.

"I'm beginning to think it wasn't written for beginners like me," Celestine added dejectedly.

It was true; the book was intended to be read by an experienced magician, or at least one who had even a smidgen of control over their gift, but poor Celestine was a clueless novice, unsure where to begin. The grimoire usually made her head spin when she tried to read it, but Queen Eileena didn't know any better.

"That's too bad, dear. I'm sure with enough time, though, you'll figure something out," Her mother reassured, placing a hand over hers.

"Thanks, mom. I've got to get going now."

"Alright, dear. I'll see you this evening."

Celestine wiped her mouth and hands clean before standing. She set the napkin back on her plate before giving her mum a small bow.

The first of her duties took her to the castle library. As princess, it was her duty to study up and one day be able to preside over official business, just as her father does. To do so, her tutor told her to read as many documents related to court business as she could, a great deal of which were stored in the castle library. It would be a pain to sift through all the documents, but Celestine was never one to back down from a challenge.

On her way, she had to walk through a hallway with windows overlooking the courtyard where her brother was training. A few moments wouldn't make or break her, so she paused and watched him.

Like every royal knight before him, he wielded Yulia's legendary enchanted sword. This sword was the thing of legends, one of her kingdom's greatest claims to fame. Supposedly, centuries ago, a former king had two sons, one born with magic, the other a normal human. The one with magic was the eldest, so he was meant to inherit the throne, while the younger was destined to become the kingdom's general. Knowing his brother would be fighting on the battlefield, the eldest desperately searched for a way to protect him, eventually turning to dark magic. He discovered a method to enchant a sword so that the wielder could not die in battle. Unaware of the risk, the eldest brother performed the ritual and successfully enchanted his brother's sword, but the price for an enchantment of that caliber was his life. The eldest brother died with the sword still in hand. A warning to all about the dangers of magic and a beautiful story of familial love.

Typically, the sword was passed on to the firstborn, but since she was gifted with magic, they made an exception. Every bearer had to learn to wield the sword, which was no small feat. It was made for a king centuries prior, so the length and weight were something they had to adjust to.

As usual, Hesperus was out sparring with the other knights, who were being taught by the captain of the royal guard. He was doing fairly well for himself, going toe to toe with his sparring partner, another one of the students, but it was clear he wasn't completely comfortable. Occasionally, his blocks were shaky, and he had to compensate. His opponent took advantage of that, overtaking him after a particularly rough rebound.

Celestine laughed. She loves her brother, but seeing him land flat on his butt was satisfying. Her eyes then wandered upward to the castle wall across the courtyard. The third floor was at eye level with her, so she glanced at the windows. That portion of the castle was rather unimportant. Vines of ivy grew up the side, obscuring large portions of the outer wall and about half the windows.

At one time, the rooms were used for the princes and princesses, but that changed after a newer, larger wing was added. Now, there was only a broom closet, the castle scholar's quarters, and the steward's room.

The steward was a rather interesting fellow. In her younger days, Celestine was almost constantly getting on his nerves. She was mostly just a typical rowdy child, but that was too much for him. She was half hoping to spot him doing something embarrassing through the window and half wishing she didn't see him at all. His beady eyes and crooked nose were practically burned into her memory. His room was the third after you rounded the corner, so

starting from the left side, she counted the windows, looking through the ivy; one, two, three, four. She paused. Once again, she counted, unsure if she had started in the wrong place or what, but again, she got the same number.

"Wait," She whispered to herself.

That hallway only had three rooms. The first two were side by side, and the third was further down the hall. Here, she was clearly looking at four evenly-spaced windows. There was only one large window in each room; none had two, so she should only be seeing three.

"How have I never noticed this?"

Had something been there before, or was she counting wrong? There was so much ivy in the way. Maybe her mind was playing tricks on her? But the more she stared, the more certain she became that there were four windows. The tiny bits of glass peaking out between the leaves shined in the sunlight, proof of its existence, and that mysterious window surely had a room on the other side of it.

Even if it was nothing more than an old, boarded-up servant's quarters, she wanted to find out. There was no way she'd get any work done with this mystery on her mind. She hurried off toward that part of the castle, her mind running with thoughts of what it could be hiding.

By the time she reached the hall, she had three working theories about what she'd find. The first was the most realistic; it was an old room that suffered fire damage and was sealed up rather than fixed, the second more wild; the corpse of a usurped king had been sealed inside, and the third returned to the practical; the floor of the room rotted, so they walled it up to prevent anyone from getting hurt.

Starting at the end of the hallway, she counted the doors. One, two, a gap, and three. Now that she thought about it, the gap didn't make sense. There shouldn't be this much dead space. Guesstimating based on the space between the first two rooms, she walked toward where the third should be, and to her surprise, she found a massive tapestry. It was comically large, reaching from floor to ceiling with an extra inch at the bottom. There were no others in the hall, making it stick out.

The tapestry was old. Celestine worried it would crumble at her touch, but her curiosity had to be sated. As gently as she could manage, she lifted the fabric from the wall, revealing the remnants of a door frame.

"I knew it!" She exclaimed, pulling the tapestry back in excitement.

In a cloud of dust, it fell, revealing the rest of the door frame and the bricks that had been used to fill it, which were lighter than all the other bricks.

"What was that noise?" The steward called, his head sticking out from his door.

"Mr. Babic! Come here," Celestine replied, waving him over.

With his typical air of arrogance, he sauntered over, glaring at her from above his spindly glasses. Seeing the tapestry on the ground, he made a sour face.

"Why have you torn this down?" He sneered.

Even now that she was older, the princess had yet to earn his respect. Around the king and queen, he was as kind and gentle as can be, but in private he still acted as though she were the obnoxious little girl he was forced to deal with.

"Look at this. There was a door hidden behind it."

Mr. Babic turned. "What of it? An old room is hardly cause for concern."

"The tapestry was covering it. It looks to me like someone was hiding it," Celestine explained, hoping to catch his interest.

"And? I read in on an old report that it was just a condemned closet."

He bent over to retrieve the tapestry, grabbing it by the frame. He was content to cover it back up again without any answers, but Celestine was not.

"Wait," She commanded, making him stop. "I would like to see what's inside. If the room can be repurposed, I see no reason to leave it closed, even if it takes some work to fix it."

She pulled out as much assertiveness as she could manage, staring him down. It looked to her like he wanted to protest, but he had no choice with her being the princess. He relented, sighing in frustration.

"Yes, Your Highness. I will return with the necessary supplies," He said, bowing as he left.

Once he was out of sight, she breathed a sigh of relief. It felt good to finally be recognized by him. She wasn't sure if she'd be able to convince him, and she was proud she did. Now, the excitement of the door's contents returned. She let her imagination run a little wild this time, unhinged by the constraints of reality.

What if a traitorous noble was sealed away inside? Could there be a secret mechanism that was too powerful for mankind to handle? Oh! What if there was a mysterious creature locked away to prevent devastation?!

She laughed to herself, knowing this was all complete insanity but enjoying the chance to be silly for once.

It took Mr. Babic a while to find someone strong enough to work on the stone and the proper tools. Celestine expected this, yet the wait was killing her. She was not strong enough, but her magic might be. With the tips she read about in the grimoire, she might be able to break in on her own and surprise Mr. Babic. It was a naïve hope, but she preferred to think positively.

There was one technique she had read about, one that could control the state of any object the user desired. It sounded simple enough: touch the object, picture how you want it to change, and speak the command, but she had never done anything like it before.

After checking to ensure no one was around, she pressed her hand against the stone and tried it. She pictured the stones in between the frame falling apart, covering the floor with debris. The book said to be as detailed as possible with your imagination, so she tried to even picture how the dust would scatter. When she felt she had done enough, she whispered her command, "crumble".

The room was silent. No satisfying grinding sounds, no shaking, nothing. She tried again with a new command, "fall apart", with the same results. Changing tactics, she started to imagine the magic inside her as though it were electricity, glowing brightly within. Then she pictured electricity surging into the bricks like a lightning bolt. That was what the grimoire had taught her, but she had never put it into practice before, and when she opened her eyes once again, she saw that her lack of experience was coming back to bite her. The bricks stood completely unchanged, mocking her with their perfection.

Thankfully, no one was around to see her blush with shame at her failure. Cutting her losses, she leaned against the wall and dejectedly waited for Mr. Babic to return.

Chapter 2

As they approached, the team that arrived to deal with the wall looked frustrated. Clearly, they thought this was all nonsense, nothing more than an attempt to humor their young princess.

They didn't expect to find anything.

"Where would you like us to clear, Your Highness?" The first worker asked.

"Right here, sir," Celestine replied, pointing to a brick within the door frame that was roughly eye level.

The worker nodded, pulling a hammer and a chisel from his bag of tools. Rather than destroying a brick, the worker aimed for the mortar in between. With the chisel in place, he hammered away. Dust and bits of mortar rained down as he dug out a small hole, no bigger than an inch across, allowing a small beam of light to show through. Putting his tools away, the worker pressed his face against the wall to look inside.

"Looks like an old service room to me," He said, completely enthused.

"Wonderful, we don't need any more of those," Mr. Babic

added sarcastically.

He and the workers went to clean up their things, satisfied that they had found nothing, but Celestine refused to leave it at that.

"Hold on, guys," She commanded, planting her face against the wall so she could see inside.

Looking straight in, she saw nothing interesting, just a floor and a small table, but when she adjusted to look to the left, she was shocked.

"It's a bedroom!" She exclaimed.

"A bedroom?"

"Yes, come here."

Celestine waved Mr. Babic over, who then took his own peek inside.

"Well, I'll be damned. It *is* a bedroom, a messy one at that," He confirmed.

"How quickly can we open this up? I want to investigate further."

"About two hours, your highness," The workers replied.

"Good, Mr. Babic. I want you to come with me to see what this room had been like according to our records and old maps of the castle."

"Yes, Your Majesty."

Mr. Babic was getting into it now, although for very different reasons. He didn't believe it was anything special, but a new room had all sorts of potential. After a quick safety inspection, he planned to put it to good use.

The two hurried off to the library, hoping to learn the history behind their discovery. Celestine went straight to the collection of old maps, quickly pulling out the massive stack of old papers bound with twine. She handed part of the stack to Mr. Babic and kept the other for herself, so they could divide the search.

"You know, the castle has had several major renovations since it was originally built. One of my ancestors designed the floor map for the west wing, added over eight hundred years ago," Mr. Babic began to prattle on.

He took any chance he had to show off his knowledge of the kingdom or his family heritage. It was nearly guaranteed every time he opened his mouth, he would find a way to stroke his own ego. Granted, his family had played a major role in Yulia's history, but to bring that up so often was a quirk that grew old quickly. Celestine had learned to ignore it, especially now that she had an intriguing mystery to solve. It was nearly an hour before either of them spoke up again.

"Huh," Mr. Babic hummed, looking at two maps he held.

"What is it?"

"This map, it's been edited," He replied.

Celestine slid over, looking at the two maps in his hands. The two looked practically identical to her, except the one on the left was more yellow and tattered.

"How can you tell?" She asked.

"Watch."

He held the two sheets up toward the window, where the midday sun was pouring in. With the papers backlit, she could see lines in the paper that were not previously visible. They were the indentations created when the initial drawing was made, and those lines had been erased at some point. The second, newer map lacked these indented lines, meaning it hadn't been edited.

"Do any of the older maps show the same marks?" Celestine asked.

"Yes, actually. Every map up until this one has been edited to remove that room, but nothing else."

While Mr. Babic pondered, Celestine began to run through possibilities in her head. There had to be some way to learn more, some way to pin down the reason.

"Who was the reigning monarch when this map was created?" She asked, pointing to the most recent, edited map.

"Let's see, this was drawn around 700 hundred years ago, which would mean it was... King Nicodemus."

Celestine gently took the map out of his hand, careful not to damage the old parchment.

"Look here, the room you are currently in is listed as royal housing for the prince. King Nicodemus had a son, Nicodemus the Second, so that was his room. The room at the end of the hall is listed as having housed the constable, and the room we use as a service closet belonged to the constable's assistant, so every bedroom on this hall belonged to high-ranking officials," She began to explain her thought process.

"That is correct."

"At this point, all the service rooms are in other hallways, and even if they weren't, why would someone erase a simple service room? It had to be a room of some significance to be situated beside the future king's and the constable's rooms. Why would someone brick up a room like that and erase its entire existence?"

"I do not know, Your Highness," Mr. Babic replied.

He had a perplexed look on his face. This was far from the simple explanation he was expecting, and from the sound of things, this was going to be a far more complicated issue than he had hoped.

The next set of documents they decided to check were the yearly reports of castle residents. It may not show where each resident stayed, but they hoped they could find an inconsistency by cross-referencing the list with the map. They hadn't gotten very far with their search when one of the workers entered, covered in dust.

"Your Highness, we have successfully cleared the entrance," He reported, bowing his head.

"Excellent, we will investigate immediately. Thank you for your work," Celestine replied, dropping the papers onto the table in front of her.

She nearly ran back to the room, and Mr. Babic had to speed walk to keep up. Her enthusiasm bordered on childlike, but she was far too excited to worry about decorum.

Just as he said, the door frame was now open, albeit a bit roughly. It was clear that the hole had been loosely carved out, leaving nasty gashes in the stone of the door frame. That was a problem for another day, however. With the new opening, she could now clearly see the bedroom and the state it was in.

She took her first step cautiously, still concerned about the potential of rotten floorboards, but when the wood held strong, she pressed on. The furniture in the room was severely outdated, with a thick layer of dust on every surface, but even with all the grime, she could tell everything in the room was of the highest quality. These were the furnishings of royalty. Next, she noticed how much of a disaster the room was.

"Goodness, it looks like a hurricane went through here," Mr. Babic commented beside her.

His assessment was spot on. Papers, clothes, and knickknacks littered the floor, some completely shattered. The bed was unmade, and several drawers were wide open, their contents hanging partly out. Whoever was here last left in a hurry.

"Mr. Babic," Celestine began.

"Yes?"

"Please return to the library and continue combing our records for any information regarding this room and its occupant. I will do my own investigation here."

"Yes, ma'am," Mr. Babic dutifully replied.

As he turned to head back to the library, he was convinced now that Celestine had been on to something. This was truly a mystery, a possible chance for him to live up to his family's legacy.

With him gone, Celestine moved into the meat of her investigation. She started at the writing desk, where several half-completed notes remained. Some had dates correlating to the reign of King Nicodemus the First but lacked any indicator of who the author had been. Moving on to the dresser, she began to pick through the clothes. Like the furniture, they were of impeccable quality, things only royalty would wear.

"Everything points to this room belonging to a member of the royal family during the reign of Nicodemus the First, but who could it have been?" Celestine mumbled to herself.

King Nicodemus only had one son, who was already accounted for, and as far as she could remember, only the immediate members of the royal family lived in the castle, with extended family having their own chalets or villas. Matter of fact, her cousin lived in a mansion in the countryside with her aunt and uncle, and it has always been that way.

Like a detective, Celestine began to catalog the information she had found and any extrapolations she had made. There were no signs of blood or of an attempt to clean up, so the murder cover-up theory was highly unlikely. It looked more like someone was hurriedly looking for things than the result of a struggle.

"Knock, knock, Your Highness," Came the chipper voice of one of the maids, whose name Celestine could not remember.

"Oh, hello."

The maid was smiling widely and had a plate of mini sandwiches in her hands. She looked around the room as she walked in, surprised to see what the princess was up to.

"Goodness, what a messy room. Should I call one of the maids to help me clean this up?"

"No need. I'm still looking through it at the moment."

"Ah, well, here's your lunch, princess."

The maid handed her the plate and bowed, but Celestine put a hand on her shoulder before she could leave.

"Would you like to join me? I'd like to chat for a minute," She said.

"Absolutely, Your Highness," The maid replied.

Celestine took a seat on the bed, and the maid pulled out the chair from the writing desk and set it up across from her. Taking a sandwich, the princess nibbled and worked to organize her thoughts.

"This room is a mystery to me. Somebody holed it up at some point, but I don't know why."

"Mr. Babic told me about that," The maid piped up.

"Yes. What bothers me though is it seems it belonged to an immediate member of the royal family, and based on the documents I've found and the clothes, I think it may have been a prince," She paused, unsure how to put the next part. "But at the time this room was in use, there was only one prince, and his room was next door."

"O-Oh," The maid mumbled, looking away.

Celestine noticed her behavior.

"Is there something you'd like to tell me?"

The maid began to fiddle with her fingers in her lap, looking uncertain. She bit her lip, thinking.

"Well, have you ever heard the legend of the forsaken prince?"

"No, I have not," Celestine replied, leaning forward.

"I don't know if I should say this-"

"Go on, I'm the princess. I need to know this."

The maid took a deep breath before beginning her story.

"My great, great something grandmother was the royal nanny centuries ago. She would raise the little Princes and Princesses so the king and queen wouldn't have to, and those babies came to be like her own. One day before she passed, she told her daughter that there was a king who had two sons, but one day, the eldest disappeared. She said everyone in the castle was told to forget him and never speak of him again. The thought of forgetting one of her precious babies was too much for her, so she told her daughter, and the story's been passed down for generations," She explained.

Celestine was shocked. How was a story like this kept from her family for this long? Even if it is just a rumor, they needed to know.

"D-Did she say anything else?" Celestine pressed her to continue.

"Hmm, I'm sure she did, but bits have gotten lost over the years. She couldn't read or write, so there's no record of it."

Noticing the shock and confusion on Celestine's face, the maid rushed to comfort her.

"Don't worry, Your Highness. It's probably just a rumor someone in the family made up as a joke. I wouldn't put any stock in it. In fact, I always figured it was just a silly fairy tale someone made up to sound interesting."

"I'd like to, but that story could explain this room," She replied, leaning back thoughtfully.

After finishing up the last of the sandwiches, Celestine gave the dirty plate back. She stood as the maid left, returning to her investigation. The documents she saw earlier, it would make sense if they were from a prince. The clothes, the furniture, and everything else lined up with the story. This room had to have belonged to a second prince who was erased from history. The question now was why.

She began to pace around the room, continuing to take everything in while processing the strange revelations. As she passed in front of the bed, her foot caught on something, nearly causing her to stumble.

"What the?" She gasped, looking down.

One of the boards was higher than the others by a tiny amount. Enough for your foot to catch on, but not enough to notice just by looking. Curious, she bent over and pulled up on the edge. The entire board lifted with ease, revealing a small portion of the subfloor, between two supporting boards filled with items. Countless pieces of paper were laid out with a couple of small boxes on top, holding them down. Being as they were under the floorboard, the papers weren't as dusty as the rest of the room, but they didn't escape the dust entirely.

"Jackpot," She whispered, bending down to take a look.

Ignoring the papers, she reached down and picked up the longest of the boxes. It was heftier than she was expecting and covered in dust, its contents shifting as she brought it closer to herself. Whatever it was sounded metallic.

Gently, she lifted the lid, half expecting bugs to come crawling out with how long it had been sitting there. As soon as the lid was clear of the box, something shot out through the gap, startling her.

"What the-?!"

The object smashed into the opposite wall, just below the windowsill, where it stayed, suspended over a foot off the ground. Celestine was so shocked she didn't know what to do. After setting the box down, she slowly approached the item, which she could now tell was an amulet. The body remained pressed against the wall while the chain dangled. The metal portion was a beautiful silver color, and the stone, a vibrant purple, was cut into a round shape with eight corners. Thanks to the box, it was shielded from the elements and maintained its beauty.

She inspected the strange piece of jewelry, checking every angle. Satisfied that it wouldn't hurt her, she grabbed the chain and pulled back. The chain went taut, and with a bit of force on her part, she pulled the Amulet's body away from the wall. She didn't pull far before letting it go, watching it return to its previous position.

"Are you trying to go somewhere?" She asked, not expecting a reply.

It appeared to her that the amulet had some sort of destination it was being pulled towards. She wondered if this resulted from an innate enchantment or a spell that someone had cast recently. Was someone currently looking for it, or was it the residual effect of someone long gone? Then it hit her.

This was her best shot to learn the story of whom the room belonged to, or at least it could lead her to a clue. She collected her thoughts and left the room with the subfloor compartment uncovered and headed toward the library. She needed to gather as much evidence as she could to help her make her case.

Chapter 3

The first chance Celestine had to talk to her parents didn't come until dinner that evening, giving her ample time to prepare her presentation. Of course, it is one thing to practice alone and another to stand in front of your parents.

The time came, and she was nearly shaking when she stood to begin. Her brother looked up when she stood, only half interested.

"Mother, Father," She began, addressing the two very professionally, like they weren't even family. "Today, I made a very shocking discovery that I would like to share with you."

Her parents said nothing, continuing to eat, but her father gestured for her to continue.

"Today, I discovered a room on the third floor of the west wing that was previously bricked up and hidden by a tapestry. Initially, we thought it was an old service room, but I still believed it required a full investigation. After breaking through the stone wall, I discovered what used to be the bedroom of a royal family member."

She paused for effect, watching the expressions of her family closely. Her mother and father listened intently, their meals abandoned, while her brother was still as blasé as before. Prince Hesperus had always viewed his sister as being more on the eccentric side. He still loved her dearly, but he tried not to get involved after being dragged around countless times for her strange whims.

"Which member?" Her father asked.

"That's the thing. There's nothing in the room to indicate the name of the former tenant. I found some official documents on the desk that suggested to me that it had to have been a prince or princess, but there was no sign of a name."

"Did you check the records?" Just as she suspected, her father asked.

It was time to show off her work. With an air of grandeur, she pulled out the maps she and Mr. Babic had found. Avoiding any food, she laid them out in front of her parents.

"See, if you look at these maps, you'll see that there is no record of the room being there," She pointed to the portion of the map where the room should have been. "But, if we go back to some of the older maps from before King Nicodemus the first, you can see indentations left behind from someone erasing the original drawing."

Her mother grabbed the maps and started looking through them, tilting them to the side so the king could see. They were both clearly intrigued, although not as excited as Celestine might have hoped.

"While looking into the matter further, I was made aware of a rumor by one of the maids."

Seeing how her parents raised their brows in doubt made her want to drop the entire conversation, but she knew if she was going to get any answers, she had to convince them. Even if it was a rumor, it needed to be investigated.

"A former royal nanny claimed that a member of the royal family was at some point expunged from the kingdom and all records," She pulled out the fanciest language she could think of. "Specifically, she claimed that a former king had two sons, but for some unknown reason, the eldest was banished. I believe that this room belonged to that son, and based on the time period relating to the maps as well as the age of the clothes and furniture in the room, my guess is that the king in question was Nicodemus the First. "

Their expressions terrified her. The thought of coming across something so interesting and exciting only to bury it again was agonizing. Her brother was listening now, a sign that maybe there was still hope.

"If this were true, what would the implications be for us? Or rather, how does this affect us in the present?" Her father questioned.

"Even if we are not directly affected, I believe the answer to this mystery is necessary, not only for our family but for the history of our kingdom as well. On top of that, if this prince went on to have children and a family, they could be lying in wait, building their power before returning to reclaim their ancestor's right to the throne."

Her response was made up on the spot, but she surprised even herself with her quick thinking. Mystery hunting was her main purpose. This was just an excuse to continue.

"Good point, you've thought of everything, haven't you?" Her mother praised.

"I have to wonder where you intend to go from here. A rumor is hardly a lead," The king interrupted.

"I agree. Thankfully, during my investigation, I came across an enchanted amulet that could lead us to the answer we seek."

A chuckle escaped her father, making Celestine freeze. Typically, laughter was a sign that her parents had stopped taking her seriously.

"I am certainly intrigued, can't say I've ever seen an enchanted amulet before," Her father began what she assumed was the denial speech. "But, as far-fetched as it seems, you made a good point. I will approve your expedition with certain specifications."

Celestine and her brother's jaws nearly dropped to the floor. There was no way they just approved her idea. That never happens.

"W-What specifications?"

"I will assign a team to accompany you, and while you are on this mission, you are not allowed to announce your presence or try to use your position for leverage. This expedition has to be stealthy."

Her mother nodded along, agreeing with the rules her husband was proposing. She couldn't think of any to add: the two of them were usually in sync like that.

"Absolutely!" Celestine cheered before curbing her enthusiasm. "I will treat this with the utmost scrutiny. For the future of the kingdom and our family, I will not fail."

"We will discuss this more tomorrow morning. For now, let's finish eating. Your food's getting cold, sweetheart," Her mother interrupted.

They went back to their meals, but the excitement and residual nervous energy made it hard for her to eat. There was still a nervous lump in her throat, so she had to swallow each bite forcefully, but at least she knew she'd be getting answers.

Chapter 3

That night, Celestine could hardly sleep. She wanted to return to the room, grab the amulet, and pull out its secrets. Her mind was running with all sorts of thoughts and theories. Who was this mysterious prince, and what happened to him? What if her first act as the future ruler was uncovering a political mystery and solving it? This could be her chance to finally break into the political sphere. Her brother had his training, and it was time she found something to which she could devote herself wholly.

The next morning came suddenly, she couldn't even remember falling asleep, but the moment she felt the sun's warmth on her face, she shot up. After putting on her finest pantsuit, she rushed to the throne room where the briefing her father warned her about would take place. When she got there, it looked like the meeting had already started without her.

In front of the thrones, a collection of castle staff stood at attention. Celestine recognized a few, but not all. It made her feel small, uninvolved, and unworthy of her position. She couldn't let that hold her back. Noticing her, the entire room straightened up, bowing and stepping aside, so she could approach her parent's thrones. She genuflected her head to the ground at their feet, not meeting their gazes.

"Princess Celestine," Her father addressed her.

She tilted her head slightly upward, still treating them with reverence. The pair looked noble and powerful. She could hardly believe they were the same people she had dinner with last night.

"As king of Yulia, I am charging you to act on my behalf for a diplomatic mission, the details of which shall remain private. Do you accept?"

Even though it was common for princes and princesses to be

sent on diplomatic missions on their own, the king was making a big show of this on purpose. It was a strategic play on his part that would benefit his daughter and show the royal family's power.

"Gladly, for the good of the kingdom," Replied Celestine.

Her parents nodded approvingly.

"To accompany you, I have selected two of our finest servants to guide and protect you. First, respected nobleman and royal scholar Auberon Fenifin."

On the right, a rather tall young man stepped forward. He had warm brown hair with pointy ears that betrayed his elfish heritage. His clothes were an elevated form of the castle scholars' uniform, blending the bland aristocratic uniform with function, complete with all sorts of devices and trinkets tucked into the pockets. He wore glasses to prevent eye strain when reading documents; when they weren't in use, he kept them on his person. Today, they were in his breast pocket. Despite his well-put-together appearance, he didn't look much older than Celestine.

"Second, the future captain of the guard, Vivian Sanford."

A young woman stepped forward. She wore a guard uniform emblazoned with the kingdom's crest. A couple of medals hung on her chest, shining almost as brilliantly as the well-maintained sword on her hip.

Neither of them looked at Celestine. Their gazes were laser-focused on the king and queen. It was a sign of respect, but still, it made her feel small. Her father rose from the throne, demanding the attention of everyone in the room. He reached under his cape and pulled out a long item wrapped in brilliant purple velvet, which Celestine recognized almost immediately.

"Our family and our kingdom smile down upon you," The

king began his speech as he approached his daughter. "With this, may you honor our legacy and pave a path for our future."

Pulling back the velvet, he revealed to the gathered audience the legendary enchanted sword of Yulia. Well, what they thought was the legendary sword. Only a privileged few know that the royal family has a collection of duplicates at their disposal. These fakes are incredibly accurate to the original, with minute differences that only the royal family would be able to recognize.

With how infamous the sword is, as long as a member of the royal family is holding a similar sword, their enemy tends to assume it's the real deal and flee. They had taken advantage of this several times, fooling countless warriors.

"It is an honor," Celestine said, lifting her arms up to accept the sword.

Her father placed it gently in her hands. She straightened up, turning to the crowd before raising the sword high. They all cheered as she slid it into the sheath on her hip.

With her business finished, Celestine exited the throne room. There were other matters to discuss during the meeting, but she did not need to be there. Besides, she had an expedition to prepare for. She was so focused as she left that she didn't realize she was being followed.

"I look forward to working with you, princess," Auberon said, announcing his presence.

Vivian was right behind him, standing tall with her hand resting nonchalantly on the butt of her sword.

"I as well. Thank you two for being so willing on such short notice."

"It is nothing. My duty is to the kingdom," Auberon replied.

This young man radiated honor and poise. He was a scholar

by trade and a socialite by passion, but he had the personality of a stuffy businessman. In contrast, Vivian had a similarly dutiful air but seemed warmer and less rigid. It was clear she took her job very seriously, yet, unlike Auberon, she didn't care about others' opinions.

"Yes, I am forever grateful."

"When shall we embark?" Vivian piped up.

"Before sunrise tomorrow. We should do our best to avoid being seen, we wouldn't want anyone following us," Celestine proposed.

"Excellent idea, princess. I will meet you in front of the stables. If you have nothing else for me, I will be seeing the two of you tomorrow," Auberon left with a bow.

With him gone, Vivian turned expectantly to Celestine. Her gaze lacked the scrutiny others had given the princess in the past. She was only a few years older than Celestine and maybe a year younger than Auberon, but she had the air of a well-seasoned veteran. To Celestine, she showed nothing besides kindness, far removed from the hardened badass she was on the field.

"I shall see you tomorrow," Celestine awkwardly mumbled.

"Same to you, princess," Vivian replied, bowing as she left.

As her father had said, the details of this mission were to remain secret. If word got out before Celestine could get a hold of the situation, things could go sour. She didn't like leaving the two of them in the dark like this, but it was necessary for their safety and her own. As soon as she was confident she had control of things, she planned to clue them in.

The amulet was right where she'd left it. No one had been allowed inside the mysterious room since the day before. It still hovered above the ground, pressed against the wall with a feverish desire to reach its destination.

"Where are you headed?" Celestine whispered, knowing jewelry can't speak.

The box it was originally in was still sitting on the ground where she dropped it. She pulled the amulet away from the wall and very carefully put it back inside, making sure she never lost her grip. To make it easier to get it out safely in the morning, she pinned a small portion of the chain under the lid, giving her something to hold onto.

She took the box back to her room, placing a heavy book on top of it, just in case. There was a lot of packing to be done before tomorrow. Not knowing what to expect, she packed light while still preparing for various situations. The staff would handle food and supplies, so all she needed on her end were clothes and her sword. Speaking of, the replica added a new problem for her consideration.

It wasn't like she couldn't use a sword, quite the opposite. Actually, she had learned to sword fight as soon as she could stay upright long enough. The problem was the replica's measurements. Her sword was an extension of herself, made to fit her perfectly and alone. Meanwhile, the replica was as close to the original as possible, a sword made for someone else.

"How does Hesperus deal with this every day?" She muttered as she awkwardly lifted the replica.

It was heavier than her own sword and about two inches longer. The design on the hilt was nearly identical, with only a slight deviation just below the guard. Her usual sword was another replica that was similar enough that no one would be able to tell the difference unless they were familiar with the real deal, but even with the replica she already had, her father had to make a show of presenting her with the "official" replica.

Word travels fast. By tomorrow morning everyone within a hundred miles will know the princess of Yulia is in possession of the legendary sword. Another layer of protection for her on her mission, and if anyone wanted to take advantage of the missing sword, they'd come to find her brother wielding the sword, as though the information they received was false. Besides, even if someone suspected there were duplicates, they could not know which was real, and who would take that chance?

Thankfully, Celestine had a second sheath she could use to carry both at all times, just in case. She'd use hers if the need arose and wave the duplicate around for safety.

Even after running around the castle to ensure everything was in place for tomorrow, Celestine couldn't sleep. She was far too excited. The amulet box seemed to mock her every time she glanced around the room. Her grimoire sat beside it. Even if her powers were pathetic, it was good to have around.

In an attempt to put herself to sleep, she began to imagine what the mysterious prince was like. He had an enchanted amulet, so either he or someone he knew was capable of magic. Magic was still illegal during his time. What was that like for him? If his friend had magic, did he ever fight for them? Was that what got him kicked out of the family? If he were the one with magic, he'd have been just like her.

She felt connected to him by the magic embedded in the amulet. Perhaps it was just wishful thinking, but having someone to relate to was exhilarating. Maybe she wouldn't be the black sheep of the family anymore.

She didn't even realize she had fallen asleep until the metallic clang of her wind-up alarm clock woke her.

"This is it!"

Like a rocket, she flew out of bed, throwing her clothes on

32

and situating her sheaths. After a quick once over in the mirror, she grabbed her bag and the box with the amulet.

"Show me your secrets, little one," She whispered before stepping out of the room.

Chapter 4

No matter how early Celestine got up, there was no beating the determination of her two traveling partners. Outside the stables, a carriage was already waiting, and two horses were hitched and ready. Auberon was at the front, checking the driver's seat to make sure they had everything he needed to steer. Vivian was at the back, strapping down the luggage. Any sense of pride she had for her own readiness was quickly deflated.

At first glance, the carriage was unsuspecting, hardly what you'd imagine royalty to travel in. Nothing on the side indicated what kingdom they were from, and even the horses were fairly standard. Everything down to the last detail had been carefully selected to ensure they could travel in secret, all before she even got up. If all of that wasn't enough, Celestine had a secret magical device that, when activated, would create a small, indestructible barrier around the user; a gift from her father.

Noticing her, Vivian straightened up into a salute. "Good morning, Your Highness."

"Good morning!"

Hearing this, Auberon turned his attention to Celestine. Going the completely formal route, Auberon chose to bow.

Being bowed to may seem like an ego boost, but Celestine has found it can be pretty awkward. Should you thank them? Tell them to stand up straight? How long is too long to stay silent? She never knew what to do and often froze up. A self-fulfilling prophecy, she was once again paralyzed.

"H-Hel-" She began, hoping to break the tension, but Auberon was already straightening back up.

Quickly, she turned the greeting into a cough and turned her head. He didn't notice, wordlessly heading back to the carriage. Before she could relax, Vivian approached from the side, gesturing to Celestine's luggage.

"May I?"

"Oh, you don't have to-"

Not listening to Celestine's request, Vivian tossed the bags over her shoulder. The princess watched, feeling completely worthless. Here she was hoping to lead this expedition while the two of them handled everything without her. She was nothing more than an investor, coming up with the idea and then having others implement. Total ego smasher.

"Whenever you are ready, princess, we may depart. All I need are directions," Auberon called from the driver's seat.

"Yes! Um, I-" Celestine paused to collect her thoughts. "I will be directing you using a magic device."

It sounded a little clunky, but it was the best way she could think to put it. Something like this had never been done in her kingdom before, or at least she had never heard of it happening. Magic had been illegal for so long this practice would have been criminal.

"Ah, dowsing, I will go whatever direction you tell me, my

35

lady," Auberon replied.

The word dowsing sounded familiar to her, but only surface level. She thought she remembered seeing it in her grimoire while flipping through, but it didn't stand out to her, so she hadn't paid it much attention.

His nonchalant response suggested to her that this was of little significance to him. Elves had always had a positive relationship with magic, a stark contrast to Yulia. Jealously bubbled up inside her.

Figuring out how to use the necklace for dowsing was the next challenge. Auberon couldn't hold the necklace while steering, and Vivian refused to let Celestine sit in the driver's seat for safety reasons. The only solution they could come up with was to have Celestine sit inside the carriage facing forward while holding the necklace. There was a small sliding window so those inside could talk to the driver, which they would use to relay directions. This way, Celestine was safe inside, where Vivian could protect her while directing Auberon.

When carefully removed the necklace the box, it snapped upward as she expected, pointing off into the distance. Vivian was shocked to see it, while Auberon was unimpressed, merely guiding the horses like normal.

"Incredible, Your Highness. Did you make it do that?" Vivian asked.

"No, I wish I could say I did, but I just found it like this. Someone else enchanted it a long time ago."

The rough and tough soldier looked adorably childish as she carefully examined the floating stone end pointing straight at her. She was seated directly across from Celestine, with the window directly behind her.

The trio passed through the bustling town just outside the

castle gate, Yulia's capital. They could hear merchants outside discussing prices with their customers. Above it all, a grain merchant could be heard shouting about how fresh his newest shipment was. "Plucked from the most verdant fields in Yulia not even a day ago!" He claimed. Auberon ignored their advertising and carefully guided the horses through the throughs of people.

"If I'm being completely transparent with you, I can't actually do much magic on my own," Celestine confided to Vivian.

Even though they had only been traveling for a short while, she felt like she could be vulnerable around the two of them. She was sure she had already shattered their expectations for her, so there was no harm in it. Besides, they were all about the same age.

"I've never seen anyone do magic before. There were all sorts of stories, but they seemed more like legends to me," Vivian explained.

"Makes sense. Magic may be legal now, but it will take time for it to return to the kingdom. Magic users aren't exactly lining up to move back into the same lands where they were slaughtered in the past."

"Excellent point, princess," Auberon piped up from the front.

Celestine wanted to ask Auberon about his past and experiences since Elves were once banned as well, but she didn't feel it was appropriate. Their acquaintanceship wasn't at that point yet. It would be rude.

"I can't wait to see what you do with magic, Princess. I just know you'll do great," Vivian praised.

"You're too kind," Celestine replied, blushing shyly.

Once they made it through the castle town, they were able to travel much faster. The further they got from the gates, the fewer people they saw on the road, until eventually, they were all alone.

For the next several hours, the trio bounced from topic to topic to keep their minds occupied. When they ran out of things to talk about, they'd slide the windows open and stare out at the surroundings until something came to mind. Despite the class difference, the three got along well, slowly breaking down any feelings of otherness they might have felt.

At nightfall, they stopped and set up camp. While Vivian gathered wood, Auberon readied the supplies to make dinner. Celestine tried to help, but the two insisted she take a seat and relax while they did their jobs. Which was probably a good thing since she couldn't cook to save her life.

After they ate, the three settled in for the night, with Vivian and Celestine curled up inside the carriage and Auberon spread out on the driver's seat. The ladies tried to convince him to join them inside; there was space on the floor after all, which was better than being outside, but he insisted. The two let it slide since he had plenty of blankets to keep him warm and the weather was fair. While not in use, Celestine put the amulet back into the box with a small portion pinned under the lid, just like she had done the night before.

In the morning, they set off once again after they'd stretched their stiff bodies. They had packed enough supplies to last a week in case they didn't find anywhere to restock, but they didn't think it would take that long. At most, they expected three or maybe four days before discovering something or giving up.

By the latter half of day two, they had reached unknown territory outside the reach of the kingdom. Celestine was fairly certain they had entered into unclaimed, independent lands between settlements, but she didn't know which specific patch. Here, there were long stretches with nothing besides wilderness, with the only sign that people had ever been there being the worn-down patch they were using as a road.

It was disheartening. She had built this trip up so much in her head, and now that reality was hitting her, she felt stupid. Vivian and Auberon didn't show any signs of exhaustion or frustration, but Celestine felt they were hiding their true feelings for her sake. She worried their attitudes would change after too many hours of combing through the endless woods.

Four days into their journey, they ran into a roadblock. They were going along smoothly when Auberon suddenly ordered the horses to halt.

"What's going on?" Celestine called.

"Sorry, Princess, but there's a mountain up ahead blocking our path," He replied.

"What?" Celestine stuck her head out of the window, and sure enough, there was a mountain in front of them.

One large mountain peak jutted out of the forest, the summit covered in snow. Trees covered the lower quarter; the rest was raw, gray rock. In the distance, she could barely make out a trodden-down path that wound up and around the side. Thinking for a moment, she remembered.

"This must be Havenspoint," She said.

"Pardon my ignorance, Princess, but what do you mean?" Vivian asked.

Celestine sighed. "Back when Yulia was still practicing their genocide, people with magic would often try to escape the kingdom. Yulian soldiers would chase them, but if they managed to make it to this mountain, the soldiers wouldn't follow. It would have taken too many resources to continue pursuing, so they had to let the magic escape. The fleeing people nicknamed it Havenspoint because of that."

Vivian made a disgusted face as she listened. In the front, Auberon said nothing. Quickly, Celestine tried to lighten the mood.

"Thank goodness that was ages ago. We'll probably be the first Yulians to see what's on the other side."

"Should we try to go around it, princess?" Auberon asked.

"No, use the paths. That is unless you think the horses or the carriage can't handle it," Celestine called back.

"They'll be fine. I brought the equipment we need if we encounter any extreme conditions," Auberon assured her.

He spurred the horses on, and the carriage once again started moving. Celestine sat back in her seat facing Vivian, who smiled warmly.

"I've never been this far out of the castle town before. I'm glad I got to see it with you, Princess," She said.

"Why would you? The town has everything you could ever need, with fresh supplies delivered often, and if you ever did need to leave, the majority of our trading partners and allied nations aren't far," Celestine replied, oblivious to the subtext.

"R-Right. I'm sure you've been to all sorts of places for royal business," Vivian played it off.

"Actually, no, I haven't. Yulian royalty has always been the standoffish type, so we don't often pay frivolous visits to other kingdoms. When the need arises, it's usually my mom and dad who go."

The mountain road was wide and well-worn, so the carriage could roll along smoothly, and the ladies could talk uninterrupted. Auberon kept an eye out for any large rocks that may have fallen onto the path, but they hadn't encountered any so far.

"If I may speak freely, that sounds lonely." Vivian said.

"Not for me. I get to enjoy the castle's libraries, practice magic, and work on my swordsmanship all I want," Celestine replied, trying to downplay how lonely her life really has been.

"But I would like for our kingdom to branch out socially. If we were to do so, we could form new relationships outside of the old ones we've been clinging to for centuries. We could even try to show the world how hard we've been working to make up for the atrocities our ancestors committed. When I'm in charge, that's one of the changes I hope to make," She added.

"Do you think you can do it?" Vivian asked, but quickly corrected. "Forgive me princess, I shouldn't doubt you."

"No, it's nothing to worry about. I understand, what you meant. I *do* have a solid plan, I just don't have enough experience under my belt or enough political support to make it happen. I am hoping that with enough time and effort, I will be able to make things right in the world," Celestine laughed, realizing how naïve her statement had to sound.

"I believe in you Princess, if anyone would be able to do it, it would be-"

Before Vivian could finish, the carriage came to an abrupt stop, jolting the two of them. They yelped as they were jostled. Celestine threw out her free hand to brace herself, keeping a firm grip on the amulet. Vivian barely moved, and as soon as the carriage stopped moving, she went to check on Celestine. After giving her a quick once over, Vivian yelled.

"What are you doing out there, Auberon?!"

She waited for a response, teeth grit with anger, but Auberon didn't answer. The two ladies listened closely and immediately heard a cacophony of animal noises. The horses whinnied in fear but were hardly audible over all the snorts and grunts.

"Auberon!" Celestine yelled.

"Stay here, Princess," Vivian ordered, pulling her sword out of its sheath and jumping out of the carriage.

Celestine tried to stop her, but Vivian was too fast. She was out before Celestine could even reach her hand out. Moments later, the sounds of swords cutting flesh rang out, intermingled with grunts, snorts, and shouts.

Many of those who routinely traveled through Havenspoint knew about the wild boar problem and planned their trips accordingly. They knew to stay away during the breeding season especially, but Celestine and her team had no idea and had unwittingly wandered into the boar's territory.

Fear paralyzed Celestine as she sat, waiting for them to return. As Princess, she was the most important member of the travel party, so it was only natural that she would stay in the carriage while they did all the dirty work, but with every moment they didn't return, her fear grew. She looked down at her sword sitting uselessly at her hip, and her mind began racing. It may be her duty to let them protect her, but she couldn't just let them die when she was fully capable of helping out. Quickly, she stuffed the amulet in its box, unsheathed her sword, and opened the carriage door.

"I'm here!" She yelled, stepping out onto the grass, ready to fight.

Auberon and Vivian had managed to take out twenty of the original twenty-five, and were working on finishing off the stragglers. They were looking a tad worse for wear but had no serious injuries.

When she opened the door and shouted, one of the boars noticed her and went charging over. Vivian, having heard her voice, turned, panicking at the sight.

"Princess!" She yelled, forgetting about the two boars she was currently taking on.

One of them took advantage of her momentary slip, slamming its head against her leg and stabbing its tusk into her calf. She shoved past it as though she didn't even notice, running over to protect Celestine.

Celestine gasped and quickly stabbed the boar in front of her. As it fell, she ran to Vivian's aid. Since her Princess was safe, Vivian turned back to killing the two boars, including the one that managed to gore her. They were dead by the time Celestine reached her.

"Are you okay?" Celestine yelled, looking down at the ugly gash on her leg.

"I'm fine. Are you alright?" Vivian replied as she got to work, checking Celestine for injuries.

"You're not fine. There's a hole in your leg," She turned, looking for Auberon, who she found a few meters away, pulling his sword from the final boar.

He turned to them, eyes going wide when he saw the blood running down Vivian's leg. He had a few cuts and scrapes himself, but nothing like Vivian's gash.

"Auberon, help me out. Grab the medical kit from the bag," Celestine ordered, dropping her sword to the ground before crouching by Vivian's leg.

Auberon did as she said, running to the back of the carriage where they kept their things. Meanwhile, Celestine wrapped both her hands around Vivian's calf, applying as much pressure as possible to stop the bleeding. Thanks to her armor, the boar's tusk penetrated a few centimeters deep, and the entry point was small.

Vivian looked down at her wordlessly without a single tear in her eye. When Celestine looked up to check on her, she looked away, blushing. Confused, Celestine went to comment, but Auberon returned with the med kit.

"Here you are, Princess," He said, crouching down by her side and opening the box.

"Thank you. Can you prep a needle for me? I'm going to stitch this up," Celestine delegated.

"Yes, Princess," Auberon quickly got to work.

"No, no, allow me, Princess. This was the result of my own incompetence, so I should be the one to fix it," Vivian tried.

"Absolutely not. You got hurt trying to protect me. Consider this repayment," Celestine chided once Auberon handed her the needle. "And go ahead and drop your sword. We're safe now."

Surprised, Vivian looked down, realizing her sword was still in her hand. She relaxed, let it drop, and then clenched her hand to brace for the sutures.

Celestine had never seen a wound as bad as this one before. Her life in the castle had been peaceful, so she did not need to even worry about things like these, but through her reading, she inevitably found out. She panicked the first time she read about a character getting injured in a book. She wanted to call for a servant to fix the problem but remembered it was just a book.

That evening, she asked her mother about it, who did her best to explain that sometimes people get hurt, but other people help that person feel better. She gave Celestine a book about first aid and medicine, which sparked a macabre interest for the young Princess. For a few months, she ate up every book she could find on medical practices, and today, that reading was paying off.

"There, all done!" She proudly said once she tied off the suture.

The stitch was crooked and a bit loose. Of course, no amount of reading can replace experience, but with how small the opening was, it would do.

"Excellent, Princess, You did wonderfully," Vivian praised.

"Well, it's a little-" Auberon began, but Vivian kicked him with her good leg. "A little too perfect. You won't even have a scar."

"Thank you, guys, and thank you again for protecting me. I had no clue this journey would be so treacherous," Celestine apologized.

"Princess, I am a knight. This is exactly what I signed up for," Vivian reassured with a laugh.

Celestine rubbed the back of her neck awkwardly.

"Still, it's my fault you must deal with this. If it weren't for my crazy ideas, we wouldn't be-"

Before she could finish, Auberon and Vivian leaned toward her with frustrated looks. She stopped talking, looking at them in confusion.

"There you go, can't have the princess apologizing all the time," Auberon smiled.

Smiling, Celestine rolled her eyes and turned away from her companions. Their constant reassurance was comforting. She was beyond grateful for their help.

With Vivian's wound tended to, the three decided to make camp early to give her some extra time to rest. Auberon built the fire for the evening, and, due to her own persistence, Celestine handled the rest. It was the least she could do for all their hard work so far.

Chapter 5

The morning of the twelfth day, while they were eating breakfast, Celestine decided to make an executive order.

"Today will be our last day of searching. I can't, in good conscience, ask the two of you to accompany me any further," She declared.

Her companions looked up at her silently. They glanced at each other, looking for a response. Auberon was the first to speak.

"If that is how you feel, princess, then alright, but I want you to know I would gladly go wherever you directed, and I think Vivian feels the same."

Vivian nodded, adding, "Yes! I would hate to see you give up on my account."

The wound on her leg was practically healed, but it wouldn't have mattered. She never once let that simple scratch hold her back.

"Thanks, you two, but I have already made my decision. Unless we find something today, I'm calling the expedition off. It would be irresponsible to sink more resources into a lead that doesn't guarantee a payoff."

The two looked at her with pity in their eyes. They knew how excited she was, and seeing her throw it all away was painful after all they had been through. However, she was the Princess, and her word was law.

Feeling awkward, Celestine hopped up and gathered her trash, wiping her hands on her pants.

"Well, I'm finished. I'll be waiting for you two in the carriage."

They nodded, getting back to their breakfast. Once inside, Celestine relaxed a little, breathing out an exhausted sigh. She was mad but more at herself than anything. Facing everyone after she pushed so hard for this was going to be humiliating, but she knew she had to keep her head high.

Grabbing the box containing the amulet, she removed her dowsing device and stared down at it, seeing her own reflection staring back at her. The bright purple gemstone glimmered in her hand, pulling against her hold even now.

"Please, tell me your story," She whispered, pressing her forehead against the cold surface.

She collected herself before her companions returned, sitting in place, looking as determined as possible to hide her self-doubt. This was it, a test of her leadership skills and their friendship.

Like the previous days, the journey was filled mostly with a sea of trees in uninhabited lands. The trio talked to pass the time. At first, the tone of the conversation was tainted by a sense of failure, but slowly, Vivian and Auberon managed to steer things to happier topics. Celestine knew what they were doing, but she appreciated the effort nonetheless. It took away the stress of the expedition. Even if they didn't find anything, she had found two allies that she believed would go far. '

They were so engrossed in their conversation that they hardly noticed the amulet move. Gradually, it had begun to drift upward. It happened so slowly that Celestine didn't feel it happening. It wasn't until Vivian pointed it out that she noticed.

"That thing is higher than earlier, isn't it?"

"Is it? Huh, could it be how I'm holding it?" Celestine asked, moving her hand to see how the necklace reacted.

The stone remained pointed forward and up. When she lowered her hand, the angle became more extreme, and when raised, the angle decreased. The amulet was raised at about a fifteen-degree angle from her hand's resting position.

"Does that mean we're getting close?" Auberon called from the front.

"Maybe? Do you see anything ahead of us that is tall? Our destination has to be high up."

Celestine was trying to do the mental math to figure out what exactly the angle meant. Their destination had to be higher than their current position, and there was probably a mathematical formula she could use to determine how far away it was, but math never was her strong suit.

"No, ma'am, the trees are so dense they block out the sky," He replied.

Sure enough, when Celestine pushed the window open, she saw how dark the forest had become. Small holes in the canopy allowed her to see the true color of the sky and the actual time of day, but besides that, no light was getting through.

"We should keep going. This is a good sign that we're getting close," Vivian suggested.

"I don't know. These woods could be dangerous if it gets any denser. If the carriage were to get stuck, we would be stranded,"

Explained Celestine.

"If I notice the conditions becoming dangerous, I will stop the carriage, Princess. I agree with Vivian. We're too close to stop now," Auberon argued.

Considering their opinions, Celestine relented, allowing them to press on. Promisingly, the amulet continued to rise at a steady pace. The energy of the trio completely shifted to excitement. Auberon gave frequent updates about the state of their path, while Vivian happily reported the amulet's angle.

After roughly two hours, the amulet was raised to about a seventy-degree angle. The forest slowly grew less dense, but the canopy continued to block out the skyline. It was infuriating.

The end of the forest finally came into view, and the trio could tell there was a clearing up ahead. It took a great deal of restraint for Auberon not to spur the horses into a run, and the ladies were starting to lean their heads out of the windows. When they finally broke through, they all gasped.

There was, in fact, a clearing like they were expecting, but instead of a flat meadow-like area like they were picturing, they found a circular space surrounding a massive tree. The trunk was easily half a mile thick, with gnarled, ancient-looking bark. Massive roots stuck out like hills atop the ground, snaking between giant boulders. Their eyes followed the trunk upward, where they found a crown like a fluffy cloud. Between the leaves, they could see tiny brown dots that looked like bridges and buildings if you looked closely enough.

"There's a town up there," Auberon exclaimed.

Celestine gasped. "Really?"

"Yes, I can see people moving around."

Elves do have better eyesight, after all. The amulet was pointing nearly straight up, a clear sign that their destination was somewhere up in the tree. However, the excitement they felt after finding their goal quickly faded when they realized they had no idea how to get there.

After finding a good spot to keep the carriage, the three got out and began to look for a way up. There were no stairs, no pulley system, nothing that could be used to get up there, but there had to be since there was a civilization up there. When they felt they had sufficiently checked that side of the tree, they began moving to the right, continuing their search. They brought the carriage and horses with them so they could keep an eye on them.

Amongst the massive stones, they began to notice large purple crystals poking out. There were few at first, but as they continued, they grew in size and even appeared in massive clusters, much like a piece of a geode.

"Incredible. What kind of stones do you think these are?" Vivian wondered aloud.

"I have no idea. The color makes me think amethyst, but I'm not well-versed in stones and crystals," Celestine offered.

Behind one of the massive stones, they could see the top of a building, which they quickly headed towards, hoping to find answers. They found what appeared to be a large store of sorts with a stable and fenced-in area on the side. On the other side of the fence, they saw a man carrying a bucket of vegetables.

"Excuse me, sir!" Auberon called out.

The man stopped, turning toward them. He watched the trio approach with their carriage and walked to the edge of the fence when they got close.

"How can I help you, travelers?" He began.

Celestine stepped forward. "Sorry to bother you, but we were wondering if there was a way to get up there?" She pointed toward the town in the tree.

"Of course," The man began, leaning casually against the fence. "I take it you've never been to Magitrea before?"

"No sir, we don't come to this region often."

While Celestine spoke with the man, Vivian, and Auberon kept an eye on their surroundings, watching for any possible threats.

"Alright, it's simple enough. You see that polished purple slab over there?" He gestured to a massive slab that seemed to be made of polished amethyst. "You hop on and tell it to rise."

"Pardon?"

The man shifted his weight, looking at them with an amused smile.

"It's enchanted. Most things in Magitrea are," He explained.

"Incredible," Celestine murmured, turning back toward the tree.

"If you need somewhere to park your carriage, I could watch it for you, for a fee, of course," The man said, gesturing towards Auberon: he had correctly identified him as the driver.

"The name's Hubert, by the way," He added as Auberon thought it over.

Celestine was so focused on the tree that she didn't respond, so Auberon took over the negotiations.

"How do we know we can trust you?"

The man chuckled. "Look around. I'm the only business around here. If I weren't honest, I wouldn't still be open now, would I?"

He was right. Auberon helped lead the horses and the carriage into the fenced-in area before tying the horses up in the stables. He inspected the facilities as he went, making sure he wasn't leaving them in poor conditions. Satisfied, he paid the man the fee and returned to his travel companions standing by the purple slab.

The instructions seemed simple enough, but was it really possible for this thing to lift them? The three stood on top of it, looking down at the smooth surface. It didn't appear to be any form of trap. In fact, it seemed pretty pedestrian. There was nothing to suggest a hidden mechanism, so maybe it really was magic? They'd never been exposed to magic of this caliber before, making it hard to believe in, but what if it was the real deal?

"Are you children heading up?" Came an old, worn-out voice from behind them.

They turned, finding a little old lady standing there with a tiny wagon pulled by a donkey. Inside the wagon were a variety of vegetables and a couple of gallons of milk.

"Y-Yes, ma'am," Celestine answered, straightening up awkwardly.

"May I catch a ride with you?"

"Absolutely."

The old lady and her donkey stepped up onto the slab. Auberon and Vivian quickly helped her lift the wagon, for which she happily thanked them. Even with the addition, there was still a good deal of room left.

When everyone had settled in, the old lady lifted her hand and said, "Rise."

Instantly, the slab began to move. Auberon, Vivian, and Celestine stumbled, unprepared for the movement, while the old lady remained steady.

The rate at which the slab rose was slow but steady, making it a pleasant ride if you ignored the insane height. As they got closer, the buildings slowly became clearer, revealing a bustling city consisting of platforms attached to branches and connected by bridges. Some platforms had buildings on top, while others had farms, market stalls, or just open spaces for people to congregate.

Once they passed the threshold into the tree's crown, the sunlight became blocked out by all the leaves, so instead, the city was lit with countless lanterns in a rainbow of colors. When they got close enough, they were able to see that there was no flame. Rather, there was a small stone inside each one that shone brighter than any fire they had ever seen.

The slab came to rest up against a long platform attached to the tree trunk, much like a dock or pier. As soon as it stopped, the old lady grabbed the donkey's reins and stepped off, leading it toward the city. The crowd was so dense that she disappeared in seconds.

Now that they were at the top, the amulet pointed straight ahead with no angle. They were in the right place. Who or what they were looking for had to be somewhere in this city.

"This is it. Keep your eyes peeled for any suspicious characters," Celestine told the others as they stepped off the platform.

Chapter 6

Countless people moved about the wooden platforms that made up Magitrea. Celestine and her traveling partners weaved in and out as space opened. They tried to inspect their surroundings as they went, but the crowd was too dense to see more than a few feet. At most, they were getting an excellent view of countless torsos.

It was so crowded that few people paid them any mind. Just in case, Celestine raised her hood to obscure her face. There was no telling how they would be received in this foreign land, so she chose to play it safe.

Gripping the amulet as hard as she could, Celestine pressed onward, leading her companions. Even when the crowd began to surge around her, she remained focused. They had made it about 200 feet into the city when the unthinkable happened.

"Ah!" Celestine yelped as someone bumped hard against her, sending her falling to the ground.

Instinctively, her hands went to brace her fall, letting go of the amulet. Even though she had wrapped it tightly around her wrist, the force of its enchantment pulled it loose. As soon as it was free, it flew forward, feverishly seeking its destination. It soared above the heads of the crowd and disappeared in a matter of seconds. Celestine could only watch helplessly. While the others rushed to her aid, she was fighting back tears.

"Celestine! Are you alright?" Auberon asked, using her name rather than her title to hide her true identity.

"I lost the amulet!"

She slammed her fist down on the ground. Vivian rushed to help her up.

Celestine squirmed in her grasp, yelling, "The mission is ruined! Without the amulet, we're screwed."

"It's alright. You didn't lose it on purpose," Vivian tried to calm her down, but Celestine was trapped in a self-deprecating spiral by then.

Her friends led her over to a bench away from the crowd. While Auberon kept an eye out, Vivian sat beside her and tried to help her calm down. It took a great deal of reasoning and a lot of reassuring back rubs to get her to finally reassess the situation.

"Alright, we don't have the amulet, but that means it must have arrived at its destination. Someone had to have either seen where it was headed or currently has it in their possession. All we have to do is find them," Celestine reasoned.

"I second that," Vivian praised.

Princess Celestine popped up from her seat with a look of determination. She had lost her guide, but this was not the end of her journey. To start, she looked around her, taking a better look at their surroundings now that they were in a less crowded area. Several buildings lined the walkways, broken up by the occasional open-air stall. The stalls were clearly the most busy businesses in the area, but she doubted they would work for gathering intel.

Moving on, she looked off into the distance. It was getting late, so a lot of businesses were closing down, giving them fewer and fewer options. What they needed was a town meeting or hangout spot. Wandering into a town meeting center would draw too much attention, so they needed to find the town hangout. Several yards away, she spotted it.

"Look over there. Is that a bar?" She pointed to a building with a steady stream of people going in and out.

"Yes, ma'am. The Rusty Tavern," Auberon answered, aided by his elven sight.

"We can ask the patrons there."

"Celestine, as your bodyguard, I must suggest that you do not announce your identity or give away any hints about who you are. If questioned, it would be best to pretend you are a private investigator," Vivian proposed as she stepped forward.

"Agreed. We are in strange territory and cannot take any risks."

With her concerns addressed, Vivian nodded, adjusting her belt and scabbard to prepare for a potential fight. Auberon did the same.

The trio then approached the bar cautiously. Celestine gripped the edge of her hood, hoping it would be enough to prevent her from being recognized, but with her two bodyguards, there was no way she'd go completely unnoticed. Celestine shoved the doors open, trying to look confident.

Inside, they found a fairly rowdy bar. The counter seats were filled, and almost all the booths and tables were taken. A few men were playing cards. Others stood playing darts. There were a couple of intoxicated patrons, nothing unusual for a bar. There was a constant din, but it was still possible to have a conversation. To start, Celestine approached the bartender.

"Excuse me, I'm looking for my missing amulet. Have you heard anything?" She began, leaning her arm on the corner of the counter.

The men in the chairs nearby looked at her, and the bartender glanced her way, but none responded to her question. Vivian and Auberon were busy with surveillance, so they weren't helping her. She decided to try again.

"I'm looking for a purple amulet; perhaps some of you have seen it. It is of great importance to my kingdom… Er, the kingdom I'm from, I mean." Her nerves got the best of her.

The bartender set his glass down roughly. "We heard you the first time, *purple eyes.*"

There was a great deal of malice in his voice. When he said it, everyone at the bar turned her way, glaring. Anyone in earshot turned as well, causing the patrons to notice something was happening. The room became silent, and all eyes were on Celestine.

"A-Apologies." She began, turning to address the entire room. "The kingdom of Yulia is currently investigating a private internal matter related to a missing purple amulet. If any of you have any details…."

Her voice trailed off as all the bravado she had managed to work up slowly dissipated. Everyone in that room looked at her with anger and animosity. She had never felt so hated in her entire life. Her companions glanced back at her, worried about how the situation had changed. Near them, a rough-looking gentleman sat up in his seat.

"Yulia wants *our* help? After everything they've done?" He growled.

The other patrons cheered. The sword of Damocles above Celestine's head was nearly visible at that point. Auberon and Vivian stood poised, ready to deal with anyone who dared attack the princess.

"Well, we-"

"Shut it, purple eyes. You have some nerve waltzing in here. Yulian royalty isn't welcome in these parts, and if you aren't careful, one of us is going to show you your place," The man continued.

At that moment, it hit her. No matter how secretive or carefully she hid her face, her eyes were a dead giveaway. She had hoped that these people were remote enough to be unaware, but they knew the stories about the purple eyes of Yulian royalty, so they sniffed her out almost immediately!

Celestine didn't know how to respond. Like a mongoose in a pit of vipers, she was trapped. How was she supposed to answer to this? She didn't expect this response and had no idea how to defend herself. From the looks of it, she'd be lucky to survive, let alone complete her mission.

"What is all this shouting about?" Came a voice from the front entrance of the tavern.

All eyes turned to the door, where a man in a hooded cloak was approaching. At the sight of him, the entire bar fell into silent revering. He removed his hood once he was in the center of the room, revealing his long red hair that fell down his back in messy waves. He turned to Celestine and her traveling partners, inspecting them closely.

"Mica, these three from Yulia say they are looking for something," The angry man from before explained.

"Oh? Travelers from Yulia, you say?"

He locked eyes with Celestine, brilliant blue staring down

piercing purple. A look of recognition passed over his face.

"Everyone, I will deal with this matter accordingly. I appreciate your patriotism, but we shouldn't provoke Yulia without reason. I understand your anger after all that kingdom did to our ancestors, but it would be irresponsible to act during a time of peace," Mica spoke to the crowd with practiced professionalism.

Celestine was in awe. With just a few words, he calmed the crowd, which was full of murderous intent. This man's leadership skills were on a level far beyond her own. He was everything she wanted to be one day.

With the crowd calmed, Mica put his hand on Celestine's shoulder and gently led her out of the tavern. Her bodyguards watched him closely, looking for any signs that he had ill intent. Outside, he looked around to find a spot to talk privately. With how busy it was, he had to lead them over to an alleyway. There, he leaned against the wall across from the trio.

"Bold move, princess, but a foolish one," He stated, crossing his arms over his chest.

"Do not insult the princess," Vivian hissed, placing her hand on the hilt of her sword.

Mica raised a brow.

"Relax. I'm just being honest, not trying to start anything. Magitrea was founded by people running from Yulia's genocide of magic."

"I'm sorry," Celestine replied in shame. "But we are investigating a matter of great importance to my family."

"Oh?"

"Yes, I can't reveal all the details, but just know that it poses a grave threat to the kingdom," Celestine offered.

He sighed, tilting his head back. For a moment, they worried he was going to dismiss or kick them out, but he straightened back up.

"Alright. I'll be on the lookout for the amulet, and if I find anything, I'll send news to Yulia. You're welcome to stay the night here, but I wouldn't recommend staying any longer. Now that your presence is known, there are some around here who would like to settle the score."

"And who are you? How do we know we can trust you?" Challenged Auberon.

"Well, I'm the mayor... sort of speak. We don't have a centralized government here, but everyone respects my opinion and listens because I've been around the longest," Mica replied.

Celestine nodded.

"Thank you. My kingdom is eternally grateful."

"Don't thank me just yet. You've still got to get through tonight," Mica stood, pulling away from the wall. "Follow me. I'll get you a room at the inn."

"Please, don't trouble yourself. We can stay in our carriage for the night," Celestine protested.

"Nonsense. After all your traveling, I'm sure you're tired of being cooped up in that old thing, so let me treat you to a good night's sleep."

He walked off nonchalantly, not even watching to make sure they were following. They scurried to catch up.

The group walked through the town like a mother hen and her chicks. Walking with Mica was a much different experience. Instead of having to weave through whenever they found room, the crowd made room for them.

Again, Celestine was struck by the authority this man exuded. Even with her status, she felt like he out-ranked her. Her traveling companions relaxed a little, confident that no one would make an attempt on their lives with Mica walking with them. Two small boys came running up to Mica, grabbing at his sleeve.

"Mica! Mica!" The first boy began.

"Hello, Harry, what seems to be the problem," Mica replied, bending down to the boys' level.

He turned back and gave the trio an apologetic look. They waved him off, duty calls after all.

"I tried to enchant my ball so it wouldn't roll too far away from me, but it keeps running off!" Harry complained.

The other boy stood behind him, watching silently, his big brown eyes glittering in wonderment.

"Let me see."

Mica took the ball, which Harry had tucked in his coat pocket. He brought it up to his face and began to inspect. Rolling it around, he checked every surface before bringing it up to his nose to sniff it.

"This is definitely enchanted. Do you remember how far you set the boundary?" He said as he handed the ball back.

"Um, 15 throws, I think."

"Ah, that's the problem. You meant to set it in paces, didn't you?" He asked.

The little boy's face twisted as he pondered the question. He lifted his hands and started counting with his fingers.

"Oh! Throws are the big ones. My bad," The realization hit him.

"It's alright. Just perform the ritual again with paces instead."

Mica straightened back up and patted the boy on the head. He waved to the shy one.

"Thank you!"

"*T-Tank you....*" The shy kid muttered.

The two ran off to fix the enchantment, giggling as they went. Mica turned to the trio.

"Sorry about that. Everyone knows I'm good at this stuff, so they bring any issues to me."

"This stuff?" Celestine questioned as they started walking again.

"Magic. I am the best out of everyone in town."

"Really? How'd you get so good?"

Celestine pressed on, wanting to hear more about that elusive practice.

"It took a lot of repetition. It helps that I'm old too, plenty of time to practice."

"How old are you?"

He turned back toward her. "Never ask someone their age."

She gulped, looking away in embarrassment. Noticing her silence, Mica turned back and gave her a cheeky grin, letting her know he was just playing.

When there wasn't a daunting crowd to swim through, the group could leisurely look around and take in the life in Magitrea. Just like the woman they saw on the platform, several people traveled with carts or baskets loaded with goods. Amidst the mostly human crowd, there were a few non-human travelers. They were from all sorts of different races and species, some of which Celestine had never seen in person before. She tried not to stare, but she could hardly hide her curiosity. Mica noticed.

"There are a few settlements nearby made up of magics that were exiled from their home kingdoms or who otherwise broke off from their motherland. Magitrea serves as a trading hub for these small budding factions," He explained.

A person with fuzzy skin like a spider and eight black eyes

on their face passed by, blinking curiously at the strangers following Mica. Celestine waved awkwardly, trying to be friendly, but as soon as the spider person saw her purple eyes, they turned away. Mica quickly got her attention.

"Because of all the different cultures and backgrounds of the people that move through here, we get to enjoy an amazingly diverse economy. These stalls on the sides of our main streets sell all sorts of wares ranging from food to potions and charms," He said, pointing to the small stalls the trio had seen previously but hadn't had a chance to inspect.

"Do you have a centralized system of currency?" Auberon asked.

"Well, we accept the usual gold and silver, but beyond that, we mostly barter. That's one of the downsides of doing business between people from such vastly different societies."

Mica explained some of the commodities that the centralized "government" of Magitrea provided, including the lights that illuminated the hanging paths. He moved on to talking about their police force when he noticed one of the lamps was out, so he detoured over to it.

"What is your favorite color, Celestine?" He asked.

"Um, teal?" She replied.

Mica nodded, lifting his hand and flicking at its center. The stone inside the lamp suddenly lit up, glowing a beautiful, vibrant teal.

"How did you do that?" Celestine asked in awe.

"Oh, it's nothing special," Mica replied as he resumed walking. "There's a small quartz crystal inside, and when exposed to the proper magic, it glows brilliantly. The spell lasts about three months, depending on the quality of the quartz and the spell caster's skill."

"Incredible. Does the quartz have to be replaced frequently?" Auberon piped up.

"As long as it doesn't break, it can continue for centuries."

The trio listened in awe. Mica explained a few more of the city's anomalies on the way to the inn. He tried to explain anything they passed that he believed would be interesting to outsiders. It was about another 20 minutes before they reached their destination.

It was a small building with two stories. The front doors swung open, hitting a bell as it went and alerting the owners. There was a small counter with a bell and a book. Behind that was a door from which a little old lady approached.

"Hello, Mica. How can I help you?" She said as soon as she made it to the counter.

"Good evening, Ethel. We have some guests with us, and I was wondering if you could give them a room."

"Anything for you. How many are there?"

"Just three."

Mica reached into his pocket and pulled out five gold coins. He set them down in front of her.

"Keep the change. I appreciate your help."

After gathering the room key and spare linens, Ethel led the trio to the room they would be staying in. Mica insisted on coming, too, saying he wanted to make sure everything was taken care of before leaving. Once there, the trio and Mica entered, and Ethel returned to the front desk after handing Celestine the key.

The trio had a large room with two beds and a chair. It would work temporarily, but an extended stay wouldn't be comfortable. Their luggage was still in the carriage, but they'd be fine for one night.

"Sorry for the modest accommodations. We don't usually see royalty around these parts." Mica stood by the door, watching them inspect their room.

"Oh no, this is fantastic. We came unannounced. It would be rude to expect you to drop everything," Celestine replied.

The others had started settling in, removing their belts, scabbards, and anything that wasn't immediately necessary.

"Hm, a humble princess? I'm glad to see it." He turned to leave. "I'll see you off in the morning. Sleep well."

"W-Wait," Celestine called out, making him turn back. "There's something else I wanted to ask."

She paused, thinking over how she wanted to word it.

"I was actually born with magic, but there's no one in the kingdom to teach me. My parents have tried in vain to help me learn, buying me books and trinkets, but nothing ever seems to help. Do you have a way to teach me?"

It was embarrassing to ask and admit her failure, but this was her best shot. With an entire city of magic users, surely there had to be at least one teacher or textbook. Mica gave her a pained look.

"A Yulian princess born with magic? You poor thing." He shifted his weight, turning back to the door. "I think I have a few books you could take with you. I'll get them tonight and bring them in the morning."

"Thank you."

A tense moment of silence passed between them. Mica had a sad, conflicted expression that she couldn't clearly see with him being turned away. His expression changed suddenly, and he straightened up.

"I'll see you all tomorrow. Sleep well."

He left before they could reply, shutting the door gently

behind himself. Now alone, the trio could assess the situation as it stood. For efficiency's sake, they talked while they got ready for bed.

"I don't know if I trust him yet," Auberon began.

"I agree. He's too nice," Vivian added as she fluffed the pillows.

"I'm not sure how I feel about him yet. He did help us out, but could that just be a trick to gain our trust?" Celestine joined the conversation.

"If we leave before we find the amulet, we could be giving him and the other residents more time to hide it or to formulate some plan to get back at Yulia," Auberon continued.

"Correct, but we won't be able to move around town freely now that our presence is known. Mica is the only one here who could give us the insider access we need."

It was frustrating, but the trio had to face the facts. They were in foreign, potentially enemy territory, so their status meant nothing. If a fight were to break out, they wouldn't stand a chance with just the three of them. Then, there was the pressing matter of the amulet. It had to be in someone's possession and the fact that they didn't know that person's intentions was terrifying.

"Well, there's nothing we can do tonight, and staying up worrying about it will only make us tired tomorrow, so let's get some rest," Celestine declared.

"Yes, Princess," They replied in unison.

Their sleeping situation was fairly similar to the carriage ride there, with Auberon prioritizing the ladies getting beds as opposed to himself. There was spare bedding in the closet, so they could at least give him a surface softer than the bare floor. After such a long day, they fell asleep quickly.

Chapter 6

Everything was silent; there was no movement in the inn, or so they thought. They were completely unaware of the intruders until they awoke to knives at their necks. The intruders hadn't made a sound. Vivian was on watch, but they moved with such speed that she blinked, and they were on her. A split second was all it took.

"Don't do anything stupid!" The first man, who had a hold on Celestine, threatened.

Her eyes shot open, looking around erratically. There were five men in total, three holding knives on their necks and two staring menacingly. They wore baggy, loose-fitting clothes in muted colors.

"We've soundproofed this room. No one will hear you if you scream," The man holding her continued.

Celestine's heart sank when she saw one of them pocketing her last resort. She thought it was a rather inconspicuous device, but these experienced criminals knew what to look for.

Auberon and Vivian had their eyes on Celestine, more concerned for her safety than the threat to their own lives. The knives against their throats were inconsequential compared to the one pressed against hers.

"You three are coming with us. I bet Yulia would pay a pretty penny to have you back," The man continued.

The man pulled her up by her hair, shoving her forward so one of the others could tie her arms behind her back. They did the same to Auberon and Vivian. With them bound, they began looking through their things, tossing them to the side so they could work unencumbered.

"If it's money you're after, I can arrange that," Celestine attempted to bargain.

"Nah, Princess, we're looking for more money than you could

provide." The leader replied.

His face lit up when he found their scabbards. He rushed to pull the swords out, inspecting every inch.

"Everyone's heard of Yulia's enchanted sword. I can't think of a single kingdom that wouldn't pay out the nose for it."

He continued inspecting them, and his face scrunched up. He'd clearly noticed all their swords were similar, but he didn't worry, tossing them and the scabbards into a sack on the back of one of the other men. He glanced around the room again, checking for anything else that might have any value.

"We're done here. Grab the brats and let's go," He ordered.

The men nodded, grabbing the trio by their restraints and dragging them along. They left through the window, lifting their prisoners over the windowsill. It was dark out; the lights from the streetlamps were far dimmer than during the day, and the streets looked nearly deserted.

Now outside, they tried making noise, but one of the men came over and performed some sort of spell.

"No one can hear you now," He laughed.

The trio were terrified as they were carried along, not knowing what was in store for them. Vivian and Auberon's minds were racing as they tried to figure out how to save the princess, even if it cost them their lives. Both of them were willing to do whatever it took to save Celestine, unaware that, at the same time, Celestine was trying to figure out a way to sacrifice herself to save them.

As they were carried along, the men made no attempts to avoid bumps. They didn't care if they jostled and jolted their prisoners. In fact, they got some sick joy out of hearing their yelps of pain as their bodies slammed against their captors when they walked across particularly bumpy boards.

Chapter 6

They didn't stop carrying them until they got to a dilapidated building near the pier-like structure they first arrived at. The floor was solid inside, but the roof and walls were riddled with holes. It looked like it may have been a textile factory at some point based on the remains of an old loom, but with how damaged everything was, it was hard to tell. The men threw them to the ground, laughing cruelly at their victory.

Chapter 7

They weren't sure how long they had been held captive. There were no clocks, and the light creeping in through the cracks in the walls could only tell them so much. The men came in and out, never speaking to their captives, only whispering amongst themselves. The stolen swords remained on a table against one of the walls, constantly guarded by at least one man. After a particular man came in to talk to the one guarding the swords, Auberon winced.

"They've found a buyer," He whispered to Celestine.

"For what?"

"The swords and you."

"How do you know?"

"I have better hearing than you," He paused, shimmying in his bonds. "Princess, listen to me closely. I'm about to make a scene, take that opportunity to run. I'll distract them as long as I can."

As discreetly as possible, he continued to wiggle. Celestine's mind was racing as she tried to come up with an alternative. It would be a minute before he fully managed to loosen his bonds, but her brain was spinning so badly she couldn't form coherent thoughts. Noticing what he was doing, Vivian began to shimmy as well, hoping to join in on the plan.

Before either of them was prepared, the door was shoved open. The trio froze in fear as the man they assumed to be the boss entered with three men trailing behind.

"Right in here, Count. One Yulian princess, as promised," He announced to the man directly behind him, gesturing to the trio.

The man in question, the count, stepped around him, looking down at the three captives. He had long, messy dark hair and gray eyes that lacked emotion. His clothes were excessive, covering most of his body in multiple layers and even obscuring the lower half of his face. The captors watched their buyer inspect the merchandise, excited to make the sale, but suddenly, the count laughed.

"Have I taught you all nothing?" He asked, turning to face the kidnappers.

Like a dog shaking itself to dry off, the count began to shake, but instead of water rolling down his back, his disguise began to melt away. Layers of clothing disappeared until he was in a much more comfortable, hooded cloak. His hair faded from black to red and gained waves. When he opened his eyes, they were now blue instead of gray.

"Mica?" The boss yelled.

The energy in the room changed instantly. All the hardened criminals straightened up in shock, grasping at their weapons in fear. The captive trio gasped.

"Did you seriously think I would allow something like this to happen in my town? I told you all provoking Yulia during this time of peace would be moronic," Mica declared.

The boss's shock turned to anger. In a blind rage, he ran to the table and grabbed the sword in the fanciest scabbard. Believing this to be the true enchanted sword out of the fakes, he unsheathed it, pointing it directly at Mica.

"Stay back! This is Yulia's sword," He threatened, hoping that would be enough to scare his enemy off.

Mica merely scoffed.

"The sword only prevents you from dying in battle; it does not guarantee a win, and even if it did, it would take more than that to beat me."

Mica lifted his arms in a flash, and a sword appeared in his hands. He vanished, instantly reappearing in front of the gang boss and slamming his sword against the Yulia fake. The only part about the sword that wasn't legit was the design and its lack of enchantment, so it was a fully functioning, fully dangerous weapon.

Once the other men registered what had happened, they rushed to help their boss, grabbing whatever weapons were closest. Many were conflicted, choosing between their boss and the man they had learned to respect from a young age, but their fear of jail time decided for them. Hoping to overwhelm him, they all rushed forward together, weapons raised high.

"Mica!" The trio screamed, thinking they were about to witness a murder.

From his position in front of the boss, multiple copies of himself radiated outward, one for all the other criminals. These duplicates ran to meet the attackers, facing off with just as much skill as the original. It was hard to keep up.

"We should help him," Celestine said, squirming in her restraints.

"Look at him. Does he look like he needs help?" Vivian pointed out.

She was right. While the original squared off against the crime boss, each of his duplicates quickly took out the other members. Many ran once they realized they were going to lose, figuring jail time was better than death, and as soon as their enemy ran, the respective duplicate disappeared, leaving not a single trace. This was half a battle and half an excuse to show off his magical prowess.

The real Mica was having a harder time scaring off the boss. He refused to go down easy, knowing he'd receive the harshest punishment out of all of them. Hoping the mythical Yulian sword would help him, he fought furiously. He was a talented swordsman even without the enchantment, but he was up against someone who had been using swords for several times longer than he'd been alive.

Their fight took them around the entire room, with Mica constantly using magic to gain an advantage. Clearly, this battle was already decided, but Mica enjoyed drawing it out. As he passed in front of the captured trio, Celestine noticed something around his neck. For a split second, as he lunged past them, only the chain was visible, but she was fairly certain she knew what it was.

At this point, Auberon managed to wiggle out of his bonds and immediately got to work freeing his friends. Vivian's bindings were worse than the other two, as the criminals had correctly identified her as the muscle of the team.

"Haha!" Mica laughed as he disarmed the boss.

The fake sword flew across the floor, and with it, the boss's bravado was sapped from his body. He looked at Mica in fear, sweat beading on his forehead. Mica held his sword up and pointed directly at the boss with a triumphant expression on his face.

"You had no chance. Even *if* that were Yulia's enchanted sword, you would have met the same fate," He declared. "Now get out of here."

He didn't have to tell him twice. Pathetically, he ran out of the building with his limbs flailing desperately, as if he thought it would make him faster. Mica just watched with a grin. When the boss was gone, he turned to the trio.

"Are you guys okay?"

"Yes, sir," Vivian and Auberon replied, but Celestine just stared at him.

He noticed this and tilted his head. She stood, walking towards him with a suspicious look on her face.

"Who are you?" She demanded.

"M-Mica?" He replied, looking confused and hurt.

Auberon and Vivian quickly jumped up, worried their princess may be treading into dangerous territory by acting so accusatory toward another political figure that *had* just saved their lives.

"Celestine-" Vivian tried to talk to her, reaching out, but Celestine shooed her hand away.

"Earlier, you spoke so confidently about my family's sword. You even pointed out the semantics involved with the enchantment."

She took a step forward, emboldened by her search for the truth.

"I did, but who hasn't heard that old legend? You learn a lot when you live as long as I have."

"Then a second ago, you told him that 'even if it were the real sword,' you would have won. How did you know it was a fake?"

74

Hearing this, Vivian and Auberon began to reconsider. She was making a good point, one they hadn't thought of until she brought it up. They thought he was just being threatening when they heard it, but now they weren't sure.

"Wh- I mean, I assumed it was a fake. I doubted you would be traveling with the real one. Was it not?" Mica faltered, taking a half step back.

"Maybe, but I saw something around your neck during that fight, and I am willing to bet it's the missing amulet I've been searching for."

Mica's expression quickly changed to rage. "Bold accusation of you, princess. To accuse me of theft-"

She cut him off. "If it's not, then just pull down the edge of your cloak and show us."

He reached up to do so, but she held a hand up to stop him.

"No magic, no tricks. I'll have Auberon check for any illusions or spells."

She was bluffing. Auberon was not talented enough to do that, but she needed Mica to believe he could so he wouldn't try anything.

"You're being ridiculous." Mica chided.

"If you have nothing to hide, just show us; otherwise, I will have to assume you are guilty. May I remind you, this would be a direct offense against Yulia?"

Faced with this, sweat began to form on Mica's forehead. Like a caged animal, he looked around the room in fear and gripped his collar like a lifeline. Finally, he sighed.

"I guess the jig is up."

Closing his eyes, he reached up with his right hand and placed two fingers next to the corner of his left eye. He then dragged those fingers across both his eyes, similar to the motion one would make if they were smearing some kind of war paint across their eyes and nose. When he reached the corner of his right eye, he put his hand down and opened them. The piercing blue they had been earlier was gone, replaced with spectacular purple.

The trio gasped in shock, even Celestine. She didn't expect he was family.

"I know, I know. Thanks for bringing back my Amulet," He said, reaching into his shirt and pulling out the jewelry.

"N-No way. You're the forsaken prince!" Celestine babbled.

"The what now?"

Celestine rushed forward, eyes practically sparkling with excitement.

"From the legend! Two brother princes, one of which was cast out-"

Mica held a hand up to silence her.

"Stop. This isn't the time or place to discuss this." He glanced around the room. "You three haven't eaten yet. I'll take you someplace nice."

He gestured for them to follow before walking toward the door. While the trio gathered their swords and anything else the criminals had taken from them, Mica repeated his earlier movement to change his eye color. This time, when he opened them, they were back to blue. Once the trio was ready, he opened the door and exited the building.

Vivian and Auberon had been wondering why Mica just let the criminals go, but they found their answer outside. A few men and women dressed very professionally, almost military, had the criminals detained. Each one was wrapped in glowing rope, the end of which was held by one of the guards. When they noticed Mica had exited, the guards paused and bowed, the criminals in their custody making nasty faces at him. It was about as effective as an ant trying to pester an elephant.

"Thank you all for your service," Mica said to the guards.

"It is a pleasure. We will take these criminals to the jail for questioning," The head guard replied.

"Excellent. I trust your judgment," Mica assured them before leaving.

He led them through town to a cute restaurant they hadn't seen yet. It was early morning, so the streets were easy to navigate. The only busy area was this restaurant. Apparently, it was the only place that served breakfast. Despite it being packed that day, the owner led them to a private room in the back. It was a luxurious space with fine chairs, paintings, and a beautiful view through the windows. After they sat down, the owner bowed respectfully and left to bring them food.

Mica barely had time to get a word in before the owner and a few employees returned and filled the table with plate after plate. They had just about every breakfast item one could think of, everything from warm, fresh bread to light veggie soups. There were plates piled high with fruits, some of which the trio didn't recognize. To round it out, the meat options were just as diverse and smelled incredible.

"Come on, I know you three have to be hungry," Mica said, ladling a bowl of soup for himself.

Faced with so much, they didn't know what to grab. After a moment of consideration, they each grabbed a plate and started sampling. Celestine reached for a particularly beautiful peach, but it floated upward before she could grab it. Confused, she looked around, finding Mica grinning with his index finger pointed upward.

"Sorry, couldn't help myself," He laughingly apologized,

lowering his finger.

The peach lowered at the same rate, landing on her plate. She stared at it, thinking once again about her mission and her life back home.

"You really are amazing at magic," She said.

"Yeah, that happens when you have 700 or so years to practice," He chuckled.

"How is that possible?" She asked

"What?"

"How are you that old? How have you lived that long?" She clarified.

"You don't know anything about magic, do you?" Mica began. "When a magician reaches a certain level of power, a level which hasn't been quantified, they become immortal. It's not easy to do. In fact, only a handful of people have pulled it off."

"That's incredible!" Celestine replied, remembering her mission.

She went silent for a moment, taking a bite of her breakfast before continuing.

"Before we came here, we found this amulet in a walled-up room back at the castle. We did some digging before coming here, and I have some clarifying questions I want to ask you."

Her tone was all business, hiding the fact that she was giddy to learn more and see how many of her guesses were correct.

"Alright, hit me, and speak freely. I've soundproofed this room for all outsiders," Mica spoke through a mouthful of soup.

While she spoke, Celestine would occasionally take bites of her meal, not wanting it to get cold. Her companions remained silent, happily enjoying the food. There was nothing they wanted to ask, and Celestine's questions took priority anyway.

"Was your father King Nicodemus the first?"

"Yes."

The first confirmation that one of her guesses had been correct.

"Were you the older or younger brother?"

"Older."

"Were you banished, or did you leave on purpose?"

"Well, I'm sure you know how Yulia was about magic at that point. My heritage meant nothing as soon as my magic manifested."

"And your younger brother went on to become king."

"Correct, which would make me your great great, something or other, uncle."

Mica grinned, propping his elbow on the table and resting his head in his hand. He looked at her with a proud smile.

"How'd you get here?"

"I walked," Mica laughed.

Celestine sighed, realizing it was a dumb question. She took a moment to eat a bit more, finding everything was just as delicious as it looked and smelled. Seeing she was taking a break, Mica did the same, enjoying some bread and soup. When they were both about three-quarters of the way through with everything they had grabbed so far, Mica spoke up.

"I've got a few questions for you now."

Celestine nodded for him to continue.

"How is Yulia handling magic now? I heard it was decriminalized, but to what extent?"

"It's much better than it was in your day. No one can be detained or punished for the practice of magic or for owning magical items or artifacts. The only crimes related to magic have to do with what the person chooses to do with it as opposed to simply being able to use it," She explained.

"I see, and your friend there. He's an elf, correct?" Mica continued, gesturing toward Auberon.

"Yes, sir."

For a second, she worried he might have some weird prejudices toward elves; he was from a different time„ after all, but he quickly proved her wrong.

"Wonderful. Elves were never allowed in Yulia when I was young. I didn't meet any until after I left. I'm so glad to see the kingdom broadening its horizons."

Auberon had been listening in as well, worried he was about to lose all respect for Mica, but hearing that, he relaxed. Even if he was from another time, Auberon was not afraid to stand up for his people. Thankfully, he didn't have to.

The restaurant owner popped his head in, respectfully, getting their attention. Mica waved him over, and the two quickly discussed the food. The owner wanted to make sure they had plenty to eat and that it was all to their liking, which Mica assured him it was. Mica offered him money, but he refused, saying serving him and his guests was an honor. With his questions answered, the owner excused himself, bowing to the group before exiting.

"Mica, I-" Celestine began, but Mica cut her off.

"That's another thing. My real name is Malachi. I changed it when I got here so people wouldn't catch on."

"Well, Malachi, I have a very serious proposition for you."

He raised a brow and leaned back in his chair, waiting.

"I don't know your current feelings about Yulia, so feel free to say no, but I am desperate for a tutor. Would you be willing to return to Yulia and teach me? I could appoint you as the royal court magician," Celestine tried to make her case.

She had previously heard that other kingdoms had royal

magicians and had always wanted to see one in person. They were highly respected, making it an attractive position.

Malachi's face sank. He looked incredibly conflicted and maybe even a little scared. For a moment, he looked away, thinking it over as he rubbed his chin with his index finger. He groaned, then sat straight up.

"Maybe it's the sentimental in me, but I could try. I've got a few things to wrap up here first, though," He replied.

"That's perfectly fine!" Celestine nearly jumped out of her seat.

Reigning in her excitement, she waited for him to continue.

"The three of you should go on and head back. Once I get everything settled, I'll meet you there."

"Sounds perfect. It should take us four or so days to get back," Celestine replied.

"Days? I can get you back there quicker than that," Malachi laughed.

"How?"

"I'll show you later. Let's go get your things first," Malachi said as he stood.

After tipping the owner, which Malachi had slipped into his pocket since he had refused to take it, the group headed toward the inn they had stayed at the night before. The innkeeper was relieved to see them when they got there, saying she had looked all over when she realized they weren't there in the morning.

She was practically tripping over herself trying to help them pack, offering them complimentary snacks and toiletries. It was all to make up for the fact that they had been kidnapped from her business, but still, they appreciated it. With that done, Malachi knew they needed to get their method of transportation but wasn't sure where or what it was.

"Did you take a carriage here?" He asked.

"Yes, sir, we left it with the man at the bottom of the tree," Answered Auberon.

"That's Hubert. He can be a bit of a pain, but he's an honest guy. I'll go with you to pick it up."

He led them back to the pier-like area they had first arrived at. A few purple slabs were floating up against the wood, similar to boats at a dock, and he gestured for them to hop on one. They did so cautiously, half expecting the stone to fall out of the sky, but they relaxed once they felt the solid surface beneath them. With everyone on, Malachi raised his right hand.

"Descend," He commanded, and the slab slowly floated down.

Even after all they had seen in Magitrea, this still amazed them. They stared in wide-eyed wonder up at the tree and town during their descent. They felt a strange, melancholy feeling tugging at their hearts as they watched it grow smaller and smaller. When they made it back to the ground, it almost didn't feel right.

The slab settled about 100 feet from Hubert's business, so they had to walk a little way. Hubert was out tending to the horses and saw them approaching, walking over to greet them. He waited, leaning against the fence like he did when they first arrived.

"Hello again, you three," He turned to Malachi. "And a pleasure to see you, Mica."

"Good to see you too, Hubert. My friends here would like to collect their carriage now," Malachi said with a smile.

Hubert nodded, walking to the back of the building. A few minutes later, he returned, leading the horses hitched to the carriage. Everything looked just as they had left it, although the horses looked like they'd been groomed, and the carriage may have even gotten a bath. Hubert opened the fence and led the horses out. After closing the gate, he gestured for one of them to inspect it.

"Never let a customer leave unless they're satisfied," He said to no one in particular.

Auberon, accompanied by Vivian, went inside the carriage and inspected everything. Celestine waited outside since she wasn't involved in most of the packing and didn't know what they all had. The duo stuck their heads out and nodded once they were positive nothing had gone missing.

"How much do we owe you?" Celestine asked Hubert.

"For Mica's friends, it's on the house. Just make sure you tell your friends," He replied with a laugh.

Malachi rolled his eyes and tossed a couple of coins at him.

"I refuse to owe anyone anything."

Hubert caught them all and sighed, assuring Malachi he didn't have to pay, but he wasn't listening anyway. Malachi was too busy looking for something. He wandered around the clearing for a little while, scanning the ground. The trio was just about to offer their help when he exclaimed he'd found it. He returned with a large stick in his hand.

They watched in confusion as Malachi used the stick to draw a large circle. Using that as a border, he drew an intricate array of shapes and symbols, none of which meant anything to Celestine or her friends. Satisfied with his drawing, he stepped away.

"Alright, drive the carriage into the circle, and you'll be back home in no time," He instructed.

"Huh?"

They had seen many weird things on this trip, but this had to be the strangest. How could a circle move them that far with any sort of speed?

"It's a teleportation array. I've already set your destination. All you have to do is drive it in," Malachi explained.

Now, *this* was something Celestine had heard of before, but she wondered if an array would be powerful enough to do what Malachi was promising. She gestured for her teammates to do as he said, then got into the carriage herself.

They waved to Malachi before leading the horses onto the array. Before they had completely entered the circle, Malachi waved and called out.

"I'll see you in a few days!"

That was the last thing they heard before the array was activated. A bright purple light flashed, blinding them, and when it disappeared, they found they were back in Yulia. As Malachi said, the array had dropped them off a few yards from the castle. Judging by the sun's position, very little, if any, time had passed.

Chapter 8

The first thing Celestine did after arriving home was report to her parents. That was only after she made sure Vivian and Auberon were able to handle putting things up on their own. Although, she suspected that even if it were too much, they wouldn't have let her help.

After asking around, she learned that her parents were currently in a meeting, so she would have to wait. This wasn't a problem. She was happy to have a moment to organize her thoughts before seeing them, and as she waited in the hall outside the meeting room, she worked through how she intended to present the situation to her parents. She rehearsed to herself, practicing her delivery and poise. With how crazy everything was, she feared she couldn't explain things calmly.

"Mom, Dad, I went out and found a magic tree, and while I was there, I met our great something or other uncle who is technically the true heir to the throne. Oh, and by the way, he's coming here in the next few days because I offered him a job," she said to herself. "Yeah, there's no way I can say all that."

What could she say to make herself sound like a well-put-together, politically-minded princess while still telling them the truth? She could always lie, but they wouldn't allow some random stranger to become the court magician out of nowhere. Omitting things would just come back to bite her in the butt. They'd surely want to get to know Malachi, and one of them would slip up somewhere along the line.

She had to make sure they understood that she had a plan, then she could introduce them to Malachi and go from there. If she led by highlighting his power and the potential benefit to the kingdom, it just might work. That would have to do, as the doors to the meeting room opened before she could think of anything else.

A collection of stuffy-looking politicians in varying states of satisfaction came pouring out. They chatted amongst themselves, discussing how the meeting went. A few cursed the world under their breath, and others happily recounted how they had gotten their way. None of them noticed her as they passed, too focused to notice the little princess.

Her mother and father were the last to exit. In one hand, her father held a stack of papers he was skimming through, and with the other, he held his wife's hand. The queen was peeking over his shoulder to glimpse what he was reading. Their expressions were neutral as they exited, but they perked up when they saw their daughter.

"Celestine!" Her mother called, letting go of her husband to run to her.

"Hello, moth-"

Celestine didn't even have time for a greeting before her mother slammed into her, arms outstretched. The hug was crushing; it had been almost a week since they last saw each other, and her poor mother had spent every second worrying about her.

Her father approached from behind, happily watching. He had been worried sick about her, but he wasn't affectionate. When her mother pulled away, Celestine turned to address him.

"I have a lot to report after that mission," She began, but her father cut her off with a wave.

"The report can wait. Let's have lunch. We haven't seen each other in a while," He said.

"Alright," The ladies replied.

He led the two of them down the hall to the smaller library typically used for receiving guests. A servant quickly noticed them and rushed over to check in. Her father asked them to fetch something to eat while Celestine and her mother got comfortable at the room's center table. He joined them a moment later.

The queen quickly started to dote on her daughter, straightening up her clothes, wiping off any dirt she found. She saw a little smidge of dirt on Celestine's cheek, so she licked her finger and wiped it off, much to Celestine's dismay.

"Mom!"

"Oh, hush. You came from me, so my germs are your germs," The queen laughingly replied.

The servant soon returned with several plates full of finger foods for them to choose from. More servants followed suit, bringing in more food than the three could ever dream of eating. They left with a bow once they'd set everything out.

They quickly got to work sampling what they'd been brought. Despite having had breakfast, Celestine found that she couldn't resist the spread and had to have a couple of finger sandwiches.

While they ate, they chatted leisurely about the trip and what they'd been up to while she was gone, but as soon as they were sufficiently caught up on each other's lives, the conversation shifted.

"So, tell me what you found during your mission," Her father said.

Celestine cleared her throat and set down her plate before she began.

"Well, after following the amulet for several days, we came across a massive, ancient tree inhabited by magic users. They called it Magitrea."

"Hm, I've never heard of such a place," Her father offered.

"From what I could tell, they keep to themselves following the genocide of magics. They seem to be a trade hub of sorts. I wasn't able to figure out their main exports, nor did I observe an army, so I believe they are a peaceful trading community, kind of like a bazaar, but on a massive scale."

Her father nodded, urging her to continue: he was fascinated by her discovery.

"The amulet led us to the unofficial leader of Magitrea; a magic user named Malachi. When he saw the amulet and myself, he revealed he'd been living under a false identity. He claimed to be a former prince of Yulia, and when he removed his disguise, I saw that he had our family's purple eyes."

She conveniently left out the part about losing the amulet and getting captured by a gang, but they didn't need to know that anyway.

"What did you do to confirm his story?" Her father asked.

"Well, he had intimate knowledge of the sword of Yulia to the point where he was able to tell mine was a fake, as you already know, only a chosen few are privy to that type of knowledge.

Based on that, I believe he is the forsaken prince from the legend the maid told us about," She explained.

The king leaned back in his seat, thinking it over. He rubbed his chin thoughtfully, processing things. He wanted to trust his daughter's judgment but knew she was still young and inexperienced. On top of that, he had the safety of an entire kingdom to consider, so for now, he had to be a king, not a father.

"This man needs to be questioned further. I'll organize a team to bring him in for questioning."

"No need!" Celestine piped up.

"Pardon?"

"I personally invited him to the castle for cross-examination under the guise that I wanted him to teach me magic," Celestine explained.

At that moment, she was so proud of herself. She had come up with the perfect excuse, making her rather impulsive decision seem cool and calculated. Watching her parents' expressions closely, she hoped they felt the same.

"That'll do. I'll work on gathering as much information as possible from the royal scholars and historians and organize a team to lead the cross-examination. You and your brother will attend. This will be a great opportunity for you to impress the court, and if he passes, I will allow him to teach you."

"Absolutely, father! I will make preparations as well. My behavior at the examination will not disappoint," Celestine declared, jumping out of her seat.

She turned, excited energy coursing through her. She went to exit the library and head off to get started, but her mother called out to stop her.

"Hold on, sweetheart. Aren't you forgetting something?" The

queen asked.

"Oh, sorry."

Celestine hurried back and gave them both a hug and kiss. With that handled, she ran out, heading off to gather what she needed to impress the nobility.

Her parents smiled with pride. The mission had gone even better than they had hoped, and it seemed their baby girl was growing up.

It was another three days before Malachi arrived. Celestine was in the middle of reading a book when a maid entered the library.

"My apologies, Your Highness, but your presence is requested in the throne room. A man was wandering around the servant's quarters looking for you," She curtsied and explained.

Celestine shot up. Today was the day, and she wasn't ready yet. She thanked the maid before running to her room to collect her papers.

In a flurry of documents and notes, she ran to the throne room. She tried her best to keep everything neat and together, but they kept sliding around. When she reached the throne room, she paused outside to reorganize everything before stepping in.

Inside, her mother and father sat on their thrones, looking down at Malachi, who stood in the center of the room with countless guards surrounding him. No weapons were drawn, but their presence alone was enough to make anyone think twice about causing trouble. The room was silent, so the door echoed loudly when she opened it, making everyone turn.

"There you are, Princess Celestine," Malachi called out to her, looking completely unbothered by the situation.

The king glared at him, making him fall silent. As Celestine approached her parents, Malachi smiled at her, and she noticed his eyes were purple today. It was a little weird, but she figured he was just attempting to let her know everything was okay. No one spoke again until she was situated safely between her mother and father.

"What were you doing wandering the grounds?" Her father asked.

"My apologies, Your Majesty, but the castle is a lot different from when I was last here. I thought I could make my way to the throne room on my own, but I got lost," Malachi explained.

"Hm," The king shifted in his seat. "My daughter has told me a great deal about you. Since you were a leader, I'm sure you'll understand my reluctance to believe you."

"Absolutely. I expected nothing less," Malachi replied.

"Before I allow you to speak privately with my daughter, you will be questioned by a collection of Yulian historians and me. Should you fail, you will be banished from Yulia."

"Wouldn't be the first time," Malachi muttered.

"I believe the courtroom is prepared. Knights escort Malachi. We will join you momentarily," The king ordered.

The knights nodded, leading Malachi away. When they noticed he was following peacefully, they relaxed a little. They couldn't let their guard down completely, but having a polite prisoner for once was nice.

Celestine's family stood and made their way to the courtroom, walking as a group. Her brother looked like he was bored out of his mind. Likely, he wasn't worried about the trial because he believed Malachi wasn't telling the truth, and if he were, nothing would come of it. He knew what it meant to have a potential contender for the throne, but he figured his family could quash the claim.

He wore a minimal set of armor and had the Yulian sword at his hip. Since he was next in line to lead the army as its general, he had to always look like a highly trained soldier, and today, he was going to show that off in the courtroom.

Her family took the back entrance, bypassing the crowd that had formed. On top of the scholars and historians summoned, a handful of high-ranking officials came to watch. When her family got into place on the raised platform at the front, with Celestine seated to her mother's right, she could finally get a view of the entire room. The seats for the public were filled with members of nobility, who were all chattering amongst themselves. The scholars and historians sat to the left and right of the royal family on a separate raised platform that wasn't as tall. On the table in front of them, they had a collection of papers and books they were flipping through. At the center of the room, Malachi stood at the pulpit for the accused, still looking completely unbothered. Celestine knew she had to make it up to him after all of this.

"Everyone! The trial will now begin," Mr. Babic yelled, silencing the room.

All attendees straightened up, and the stragglers standing around the door hurried to their seats. Once everything was settled, the king stood.

"Malachi, you stand here today because you claim to be a forgotten member of the royal family of Yulia. Before the cross-examination begins, is there anything you want to say?"

"No, sir," Malachi replied.

The king nodded, then sat back down. A man from the group of historians stood next. He bowed to the king and queen before turning to address Malachi and the rest of the courtroom.

"Tell me which king was your father," He said.

"King Nicodemus the first, 38th king of Yulia," Malachi replied.

"And your mother?"

"His first wife, Queen Anna."

Celestine looked around and noticed the perplexed looks on the audience's faces. With everything Malachi said, the historians would go flipping through their documents to double-check. Another historian raised his hand once the first stopped. The original sat down while the second historian stood with a document.

"During King Nicodemus's reign, who was the steward?" He asked.

A peculiar question, but when you think about it, only someone who had been there or had access to ancient records would have been able to answer that. Stewards don't receive much praise outside of their castle.

"Mr. Sliver, but he was replaced by Mr. Campbell after he hurt his back," Malachi answered.

The scholars and historians began to whisper amongst themselves. The gathered nobility watched closely, wishing they could hear their secret conversations. A third man stood, this time a scholar, as evident by the robes he wore.

"Mr. Malachi, as everyone knows, the royal family of Yulia is marked by their purple eyes, a gift from god to help them see beyond the masses and lead our people to a bright future. Yes, your eyes are purple, but you are also a prolific magic user. We have in our possession, the Mirror of Everlasting Truth. Would you be willing to stand before it?" The man asked.

"Absolutely," Replied Malachi.

The scholar nodded, gesturing for one of the knights standing off to the side to bring the mirror. Ironically, the kingdom of

Yulia was adamant about banishing magic and all magical items, except when it came to things that could benefit them. For example, the Mirror of Everlasting Truth was gifted to a king centuries prior by an allied monarch. The mirror reflected nothing but the truth, meaning if someone had transformed or were hiding behind an illusion, it would show in their reflection. The king accepted the gift and began to use it to expose magic users and test for spies. Why that wasn't considered using magic was nothing more than royal privilege.

As Celestine watched the knight bring the mirror in, she noticed Vivian standing guard by one of the doors. Not far from her, Auberon sat among the guests in the crowd. She wondered if maybe they were invited to be potential witnesses or if they were just doing their jobs.

The knight set the mirror in front of Malachi at an angle so the king and queen could see it, then bowed to the court. There was a large silk sheet to cover the surface and protect it from scratches, so no one could see the reflection just yet. After straightening up, the knight removed the sheet with a flourish, revealing the extravagant silver mirror beneath.

The face was easily four feet tall, two feet wide, and the stand added another foot or two. Beautiful filigree framed the outer edges, adding another 3 to 4 inches all around. It was an imposing piece, the kind of thing only royalty would own.

The entire room leaned forward to get a good look. Reflected in the mirror, Malachi looked exactly the same. His eyes were still the same shade of purple he claimed them to be. Celestine breathed a sigh of relief now that she knew her intuition was correct. Had she been wrong, she never would have recovered from the shame.

No one spoke again until the mirror had been removed.

Surprisingly, it was her father that posed the next question.

"Why did you leave the kingdom?"

Malachi's face sank for a small, hardly perceptible moment, but he was quick to recover.

"As a magic user, I wasn't welcome here. My father banished me and, from the sound of it, removed me from the kingdom's history to cover up the fact that his son had magic," Malachi explained.

The king nodded, satisfied with his answer, and the next person stood to ask a question.

"Name the largest farm owner during your father's reign."

"Easy, Mr. Niadric, he had the most amazing apple orchards."

"What was the kingdom's main export?"

"Well, when I was little, it was wheat, but right before I left, there was a series of bad harvest seasons, so they switched to legumes."

Celestine remembered reading in her history book about the bad wheat harvests during King Nicodemus's reign. It nearly crippled the kingdom, but by switching to legumes, they were able to continue producing crops and rejuvenate the soil.

"Who was your royal nanny?"

"Sweet Miss Cindy. We were all so excited when she had her daughter, but we hated to lose her as a nanny."

The king, without standing, posed his next question.

"At your coming-of-age party, what did your father give you?"

"A cape, he said it made me look like a real king."

The king smiled, picturing a similar situation between him and his daughter. He stood suddenly, making the entire courtroom turn to him.

"Your story is compelling, but I believe no amount of questioning will prove it. There is no record of your existence, and you cannot provide any solid evidence. I had hoped that by asking these questions, we could confirm or deny your claims, but the more we go on, the more I realize that you could be telling the truth or you could just be a well-informed liar. If only there was a document or some other piece of hard evidence, but the only document that could possibly provide an honest, unbiased answer would be the personal journals of someone from that time who didn't want to contribute to your eradication. However, the journals of King Nicodemus the first and second have never been found."

Malachi raised his hand, and the king gestured for him to speak.

"Apologies, I didn't want to interrupt you, but you said my brother's journal is missing. I might know where to find it," Malachi explained.

"Really? Why is that?" The king asked.

"My brother and I used to keep all sorts of secrets. One could say we were partners in crime, and I knew all of his hiding spots. If that journal hasn't completely fallen apart by now, I can find it."

After a moment, the king looked up to address the entirety of the court.

"Everyone, thank you for coming out here to provide your expertise and protect the kingdom, but it appears that this is an internal matter. I will be tasking Princess Celestine and Prince Hesperus with further investigation. Court is now dismissed," He commanded.

He turned and began to walk away, his family hurriedly following behind. Immediately, the gathered crowd began to chat amongst themselves once again. Once they exited the courtroom, they'd discuss theories and ideas, but while they were still within earshot of those involved, they kept it to themselves.

Celestine was frustrated that she never got a chance to pull out her documents but happy that Malachi seemed to have a shot at proving himself. She followed her father through the back entrance they had used prior, waiting for him to give her the orders for the investigation. It wasn't until they were well beyond the view from the courtroom that he finally addressed her.

"Celestine, Hesperus," He began. "So far, I have seen nothing to make me doubt this man, but we cannot just take his word for it. The two of you are to take him to where he claims the journal is, but if, at any point, his behavior comes across as suspicious or dangerous, you are to kill him without hesitation. Have I made myself clear?"

Celestine gulped, feeling the weight of her father's words. She had never taken a life before, nor was she prepared to do so. On the other hand, her brother had been training since he was young and had no reservations about killing.

"Yes, father," He said, bowing to the king.

"Y-Yes, father," Celestine spoke up, bowing as well.

"Good. I suggest you take another knight or two, just in case. His abilities with magic will make him a formidable fighter," Her father added.

Immediately, Vivian and Auberon came to her mind. The two had already proved their skill and devotion to her, so they would be perfect. Not to mention the fact that personally assisting the princess would be extremely prestigious for them. It could even lead to a promotion, and she owed them for all of their help.

"I trust that the two of you will make the best decision for this kingdom, so I will support you no matter what you decide."

With that, their father left, heading off to return to his duties. The queen followed close behind, giving her kids a bright smile as she passed. Once they were gone, Hesperus turned to his sister.

"Alright, let's go escort the crazy man around," He sighed.

Chapter 9

Celestine and Hesperus returned to the courtroom to retrieve Malachi, weaving through the crowd of people exiting. They found him standing exactly where he'd been prior and watching everyone exit. When he noticed their approach, he smiled.

"There you are, Princess," He greeted.

A couple of knights stood beside him still, but they stepped aside respectfully when they noticed the Prince and Princess.

"Hello, Malachi. Sorry about all of that."

"Ah, don't be. I expected as much. Your father would be a foolish king if he believed every story he heard," Malachi replied with a grin.

"Alright, enough with the pleasantries. Lead us to where you believe the journal is so we can get this over with," Interrupted Hesperus.

He stood with his hand on his hip, glaring at Malachi. He was displaying more bravado than usual, partly because he was on a special mission from his father and partly because he wanted to intimidate this mysterious stranger.

"Straight to the point, I see. Okay, if the two of you would follow me," Malachi replied.

The two nodded, following close behind him as he began to walk off. He confidently exited the courtroom and then turned, starting down the adjacent hallway. By now, most of the audience for the trial had left, leaving only knights and other castle staff who milled about. Seeing them, Celestine remembered the two assistants they were meant to recruit.

"Hold on, you two," She said before running off.

She checked every group of knights she could find, scanning for Vivian or Auberon. Everyone she saw greeted her politely, and she returned their sentiments with a quick "hello" before moving on. It wasn't until she checked one of the side entrances to the courtroom that she found them.

Vivian was leaning against the wall while Auberon stood explaining something to her. Occasionally, he would make gestures with his hands, turning away illustratively. It was during one of these turns that he spotted Celestine. Seeing his expression, Vivian turned too.

"Your Highness," The two greeted as they bowed.

"Are you two free right now? I need your help with something," She asked.

The duo straightened up, pausing to think about it.

"I can make time. What do you need?" Auberon began.

"Same here," Vivian added.

"I need the two of you to accompany my brother and me to escort Malachi."

"Absolutely. Was hoping to see him again anyway," Auberon replied.

Vivian nodded.

"Thank you guys so much. I owe you."

The two smiled. It was sweet that Celestine valued their help so much, but she was the princess. They had to do whatever she wanted.

They followed her as she led them back to where she'd left Malachi and her brother. As they got closer, they could hear that the two were in the middle of a conversation. They were facing away, so Celestine couldn't hear clearly, but she did hear Hesperus laughing.

"And then?"

"I had to rebuild the entire thing! Took me a week at least," Malachi laughed, noticing the trio.

"Sorry about that," Celestine apologized for interrupting the story.

"No worries. If that's everything we need, we can get going."

"Yes, lead the way," Celestine gestured for him to lead.

He nodded, turning back the way he was headed earlier. The others followed close behind. Celestine glanced over and noticed her brother looked much more relaxed than he had earlier, likely due to their conversation earlier. He put on an air that was rigid and professional but not as aggressive as before.

The group followed Malachi down several hallways, watching to ensure he wasn't up to anything. From what they could tell, he was just walking and taking in his surroundings, looking at everything that had changed since he left. He turned a corner and suddenly stopped.

"Wait, this didn't use to be here," He said, pointing to a wall ahead.

"Yeah, a portion of the castle was damaged during a storm, so it was demolished," Auberon explained.

"Huh."

Malachi stood there with a confused expression.

"If you tell me where we're headed, I can help us get there," Celestine offered.

"Well, I was hoping I could do it on my own. It would be a bit embarrassing if I had to have someone lead me around my old home," He chuckled.

"No worries. A lot has changed. There's nothing to be ashamed about."

"Alright. I'm trying to get to my old room."

"Gotcha. If you'll follow me, I'll have us there in no time," Celestine said as she led the way.

He looked a bit disheartened, but he followed her anyway, falling in place behind her along with Vivian and Auberon. Her brother made sure to walk by her side, flaunting his status a little bit.

Malachi hadn't been too far off, so they didn't have to walk very long before they got to his hallway. When they were only a few meters from his old room, Malachi's face lit up.

"Look at this place. I can't believe how much it's changed!" He exclaimed, spinning around to get the whole view.

He had a huge grin, loving all the memories the place was bringing back. When his eyes came to rest on the entryway to his room, specifically the missing door, he stopped. His demeanor changed instantly. It was like the light inside of him had been sucked out. The others noticed, looking up at him in concern. Seeing they were looking, Malachi perked up.

"Let's get that journal," He said, heading toward the door.

Despite his tone, Celestine still noticed the way his shoulders were drooping. The group followed him to the threshold, where Vivian and Auberon stopped.

"We'll stay here, princess. If you need us, you can call," Vivian said, gesturing between Auberon and herself.

Chapter 9

"Are you sure?" Celestine asked.

"Yeah. That room's not that big. It'd get crowded. Besides, this is a family matter," Vivian explained.

Celestine glanced at Auberon, who nodded in agreement.

"Alright. Keep an eye out for us."

"Yes, princess."

Turning back, she realized Malachi and Hesperus had already entered, so she hurried off to join them. Malachi was wandering around the room inspecting things while Hesperus stood off to the side. Her brother was mostly looking around the room in bored curiosity, occasionally glancing over at their prisoner to make sure he kept an eye on him. He scowled down at the dust, disgusted by the state of it.

Malachi walked purposelessly around the room, looking at the state of everything. The room was still in complete disarray and covered with dust: Celestine told the maids not to clean it as the investigation was still ongoing.

"I'm surprised. Everything is just how I left it," Malachi commented as he touched some of the clothes hanging out of their drawers.

"Wait, you did this?" Celestine asked.

"Yup. I was in a rush to get out of here, so I tore through everything," He explained.

He wasn't hiding his feelings now. It looked as though he was mourning as he wandered the room. Not knowing how to comfort him, Celestine stood there awkwardly watching. Hesperus was lucky not to be paying close enough attention to feel the tenseness.

"Sorry to rush you, but could we hurry up and get this book?" Hesperus spoke up, breaking the silence.

"Oh, yes. One moment," Malachi said as he snapped out of it.

He walked over to the wall adjacent to the room that used to belong to his brother. The wall was made of old bricks covered in a thin layer of white paint that had begun to deteriorate. Starting from the outer wall, he counted the bricks, moving inward. Then, once he found the right spot, he started counting, moving up from the floor. Finally, he settled on a roughly centered brick and maybe three feet from the floor. He reached up and pulled it out.

Behind the brick, there was a small space between the two rooms. It looked as though someone had removed one of the bricks that had made up the inner portion of the wall, leaving a convenient little hiding spot. Malachi reached in and pulled out two dusty, ancient-looking journals.

"Nicky was always predictable," Malachi said with a smile as he looked down at them.

This entire hallway had been renovated at some point for better insulation and to replace the paint. That meant that the bricks on the other side of the wall had been resealed, making it nearly impossible to remove them. That had to be why no one had found the journals previously.

"Are they intact?" Celestine asked, walking over to inspect.

"Looks like it." Malachi opened one of the journals carefully, afraid it might crumble at his touch.

Surprisingly, it held up. Inside, the pages were yellowed and tattered, but the writing was still legible. She was amazed. Most of the kings' journals had been meticulously preserved or replicated; yet, there was one hidden inside a wall without any extra protection. It was like finding untarnished gold inside a tree trunk. When he closed the book, Malachi passed the two journals to Hesperus.

"Here you go. Your father will probably want these to be

authenticated and placed before the Mirror of Everlasting Truth," He explained.

"Alright. I'm going to deliver these. Celestine, are you coming with?" Hesperus asked.

"Um, I'll stay here with Malachi and keep an eye on him. With Vivian and Auberon standing guard, I should be fine."

Hesperus nodded.

"Alright. I'll have someone notify you if there are any developments," He said before turning and leaving.

Vivian and Auberon glanced inside after he left, ensuring Celestine was on her own before returning to guard duty.

With the journals retrieved, Malachi slid the brick back in place, his hand lingering on the wall. The awkward atmosphere was back, and Celestine didn't know what to say again. She was about to speak up when Malachi beat her to it.

"My brother and I used this little gap as our own secret tunnel. At night, we would remove the bricks and talk when we were supposed to be asleep. If one of us was in trouble, the other would sneak treats through it."

There was sadness in his tone. For the first time since she had met him, she felt like he was opening up to her.

"That was really sweet of the two of you," She complimented.

"Yeah. We tried really hard to look out for each other," He continued. "I was his big brother. It was my job to protect him. That's why I enchanted his sword."

"Wait, you're the one who enchanted the sword?" Celestine asked, half surprised. Honestly, she had started to suspect it because of the similarities to the old story.

He nodded. "Yes, I worked so hard to figure out how to do that, but when I went through it, the process took so much out of me that I was out for days."

He laughed, remembering the experience, but his laughter and smile quickly faded as reality hit him again. Malachi turned, walking over to his old desk. He placed a hand on the seat's backrest, gazing down at the papers still strewn about.

"I'm sorry. This is bringing back a lot of memories for me," He apologized.

"No, no! I'm happy to listen if you need it," Celestine reassured him.

"Thank you. I knew my brother died; he wasn't magic like me, and I had been refusing to face the reality of it. As long as I didn't think about it, I was okay, but now that I'm here, I can't run anymore."

Sighing, Malachi walked over and plopped onto the bed, causing a massive dust cloud. Celestine was too close, getting a mouthful of dust that sent her into a coughing fit. When she could finally breathe again, she looked at Malachi lying face down on the bed and couldn't help but chuckle.

She walked over and sat on the edge, looking down at him. It reminded her a lot of the times she threw herself on her bed after a particularly frustrating day. He spent a while just laying there motionlessly, but then he lifted his head, propping it up with his hands.

"This is gonna be a tough one, kiddo. I've got a lot of baggage," He sighed, eyes closed.

"That's alright. I'm sure we can work through it together," Celestine offered.

Malachi opened one eye and looked at her curiously. Then, he grinned.

"We're going to have a lot of fun. Do you mind if I clean my room? I'm tired of all the dust," He asked.

"Sure. Now that we're done with the journal business," She

replied.

He hopped up, moving his limbs dramatically as he walked away from the bed. It was the sort of movement you did when you were trying to act unbothered and confident when, in reality, you weren't sure if you should laugh or cry.

Stopping in front of his desk, he rolled up his sleeves and adjusted his footing before harshly flicking his hands as though he were shooing away a fly. A strong gust of wind blew, blowing the dust away and sending the papers flying. Celestine watched in wonder as the papers then fluttered back toward the desk, organizing themselves into neat, orderly piles. Even the writing implements that had been scattered around reoriented themselves. Vivian stuck her head inside the door as Malachi stood admiring his handiwork.

"Princess, is everything alright?" She asked, having heard the wind.

"Yes. Sorry, the two of you can go now. I should be able to handle this," Celestine replied, standing to address them.

"Actually, I think one of us should stay, just in case," Auberon piped up.

Vivian nodded in agreement.

"Oh, alright. I appreciate that. You two can decide who stays."

"I will. It's a knight's duty to always protect their princess," Vivian offered.

"That works for me. I've got some paperwork I need to get caught up on," Auberon said before turning to Celestine. "Good luck, Princess."

After giving a poised and perfect bow, he turned and left. Vivian turned to resume her place outside the door, but Celestine put a hand on her shoulder to stop her.

"You can come inside. There's no need for you to stay out

there," She explained.

"Yeah, I don't mind you-" Malachi began as he went to pass in front of his bed but was interrupted when his foot hit a loose board sitting on the floor, nearly causing him to trip.

Celestine and Vivian cried out in concern, running over to check on him. Malachi held a hand up to let them know he was alright, but his focus was on the board. It was one of the floorboards, he could tell. He just didn't know where it came from. Celestine instantly recognized it as the board she had removed when she found the amulet.

"Where did this..." Malachi muttered to himself as he looked around.

His eyes locked on the open portion of the floor. Moving over slightly, he could see how deep the opening was and what was inside, and he realized it was his old hiding spot. Instantly, his face went bright red.

"I-I didn't realize I left the amulet there," He babbled.

"Sorry, I should have put the board back," Celestine apologized, incorrectly assuming that was why he was so worked up.

"Um, how much did you see in there?" He asked.

"Pardon?"

"Did you look through anything else?"

"Oh, no. The amulet was on top, and once I got it, I moved on," Celestine explained.

Malachi relaxed.

"Good, good."

He bent over and grabbed the board, moving it back into place and covering the hiding spot. The girls watched him, all too aware of his awkward behavior. They glanced at each other, not sure what to do. When he straightened back up, he noticed them staring before they could turn away. He had to give them some explanation, or they'd be curious forever.

"Sorry. That's just some really..... personal stuff," He began, rubbing the back of his neck. "I'm not exactly ready to talk about it yet."

"That's alright. We don't have to know if you don't want us to," Celestine replied.

He gave her a bright smile, appreciating her understanding.

"Maybe one day, but for now, I'm not ready."

The ladies nodded, letting him get back to his cleaning. Just like he did with the desk, he walked around waving at different sections of the room, sending the dust flying. If any items were on the floor or hanging out of drawers, they moved on their own until they were back in place. Celestine and Vivian stood to the side to stay out of his way. They were amazed by how easily he could perform such a feat of magic. He wasn't even breaking a sweat as he did something Celestine could only dream of in her current state.

When he got to the window, which had cracks in the glass and crumbling stones around the frame, he made a different gesture. The dust dispersed, and then the cracks slowly began to close. The broken stones seemed to regrow the missing, crumbled pieces until they looked as flawless as the day they were made.

"Amazing!" Vivian remarked.

"What? The window?" Malachi turned around, having already moved on.

"Yes, sir! I've never seen someone repair stones with magic."

"Ah, that was nothing. I teleported the three of you and your carriage, remember? That was more of a feat than this," Malachi said as he looked over the room, checking for any spots he might have missed.

"Still, I'm amazed. I may sound silly, but I've never been able to see magic up close like this before. No one in my family has it, and there are very few citizens who practice it," she explained.

"Well, now that I'm here, you'll be seeing all sorts. Someday, you'll even get to see Celestine performing magic," He laughed.

Vivian looked over and smiled at Celestine, making her turn away and blush. Malachi walked over and hopped onto the bed again, the sound of creaking wood making the ladies turn back and interrupt their moment. He tucked his arms behind his head, relaxing.

The ladies walked over toward the desk. Celestine took a seat in the desk chair, and Vivian leaned against the bed facing her. Malachi shut his eyes, fully relaxing and letting them have some time to themselves.

"I don't know how long it's going to take to get the journal authenticated, and even then, we'll probably have to have someone keeping an eye on him for a little while as a formality. Long story short, I don't want to keep you from your responsibilities," Celestine began.

"Don't worry, for you, Princess, there is nothing more important," Vivian replied.

"Yes, well, thank you. Tonight, I think I'll station two guards wearing enchanted armor outside his room. We should have an answer about the journal by tomorrow," Celestine spoke more to herself than anyone.

Malachi half listened to their conversation, unbothered by it. He was confident that the journal would clear his name; if it didn't, he would have no trouble escaping. When he opened his eyes again, he noticed that the light streaming in through his window was growing dim.

"If you're going to get guards, you probably want to go ahead and do so. Wait too much longer, and it'll be dark," He spoke up.

The princess turned, noticing how much darker it had gotten in there. She jumped to her feet.

"Indeed, I'll-"

Vivian cut her off, stepping in front of her.

"Allow me, princess. Stay here and keep an eye on him for me?"

Celestine thought for a moment, then nodded, agreeing to her plan. Vivian grinned as she ran off to find available guards. Malachi and Celestine watched her go, and once she was out of sight, Celestine took a seat.

She turned back to Malachi, who was curiously looking her way. He maintained eye contact, waiting for her to say something, but she remained silent. Realizing she wasn't going to say anything, he spoke up.

"Thanks for all the work you're doing. I'll start teaching you once we get everything sorted out."

"It's no problem. We're family, after all," She replied.

"Do you have any goals with magic? I can tailor my lessons to meet your needs," He offered.

"No, but I have a plan for you as my royal magician."

"Do tell," He said with an excited grin.

Celestine sat up straight, moving the chair closer to the bed.

"There's a contest held once a year in the kingdom of Viridisia where nations bring their royal magicians to show off their power. Yulia has never participated, and I thought it would be a historical event if I took you there. A chance for us as a kingdom to show the kind of power we now have while also getting my name out there."

"I like it. You sure have put a lot of thought into this," Malachi replied.

"Yes, I've been looking for any chance to prove myself, and I want to fix our kingdom's relationship with magic," Celestine declared with a brave, determined look.

"I did, too," Malachi sighed.

Before he could elaborate, Vivian returned with two guards.

"Here you go, Princess. These two are going to be the first on shift. I have to get them a set of enchanted armor, but you're welcome to go ahead and leave," She explained.

"Thank you, Vivian, and thank you two for your service," Celestine said as she got up to greet them.

Malachi remained in place, watching the interaction. Celestine turned back to him, wanting to continue the conversation from earlier, but he waved her off.

"Go to sleep, Princess. We've got a lot of work ahead of us, so you'll need all the rest you can get," He said.

"Alright. We'll work on getting you a door soon," Celestine laughed, gesturing to the door frame as she stepped through it.

"Don't worry about it. I'll make myself one. For now, having it open will help the guards keep an eye on me," Malachi joked.

Vivian and the two knights heard and half chuckled. On that note, Celestine said her goodbyes and left.

As she walked back to her room, she kept thinking about his words. There was still so much about his past that she didn't know. She had full trust in him, but she worried he was hiding things to spare her. She pushed those thoughts away, focusing on her plans for the contest as she went to bed.

Chapter 10

In the morning, before Celestine even had time to get dressed, a servant knocked on her door. After wiping the sleep from her eyes, she straightened up her pajamas and went to see what the visitor needed. She found a small, round-faced maid standing just outside her room.

"Good morning, Princess," She began with a bow. " Your father has requested you meet him in the west wing library."

"Alright. I'll get ready and grab a bite or-"

Celestine went to shut the door, but the maid raised her hand to stop her.

"Apologies, Princess! We are making arrangements to serve breakfast in the library, so please go as soon as you are dressed," She added.

"Ah, thank you. I was thinking about making a detour, so that saves me a trip," Celestine laughed.

After shutting the door, she dressed as quickly as possible in one of her favorite outfits. She topped it off with her sword and scabbard. With a quick once over in the mirror, she took off toward the library.

The hallways were mostly empty as she passed through. It was still early in the morning, so most of the castle residents hadn't gotten up yet. When she reached the hall the library was on, she saw a group of soldiers guarding the entrance. The door was open, and she could see light streaming from within. The soldiers stepped aside to allow her entry.

"There you are, Celestine," Her mother beamed once she saw her.

The king and queen were sat at the center table, snacking on the array of finger foods the staff had brought. The queen was sipping leisurely on a cup of tea. Her father was working on his second cup of coffee and snacking on some tea cakes.

"Good morning," Celestine greeted formally, taking her seat. "May I ask why I've been called here this morning?"

She grabbed the pitcher of tea, pouring herself a cup as she waited for the answer. Her father finished chewing before answering.

"We need to discuss the results of the journal investigation. However, we are waiting for one more guest."

"May I know the consensus?"

If she was wrong and Malachi was an imposter, she wouldn't see any major punishment thanks to her status, but it would still be a crippling blow to her image.

"Not yet. I would rather not repeat myself," He laughed, which she hoped was a sign he was in a good mood.

The sound of approaching footsteps cut off her attempt to continue the conversation. The three of them turned to the door as the visitors entered. Malachi, followed by two guards wearing magic-resistant armor. He had a bright smile and strode confidently into the room midway through a conversation with one of the guards.

"Pardon me, your majesties," He said, turning from the guards and addressing Celestine and her parents.

"Good morning, Malachi. Guards, return to your post," The king commanded.

The guards bowed, leaving their prisoner in the capable hands of the royal family and their attendants. The king gestured for Malachi to sit next to Celestine, which he did.

"Would you like something to eat?" The queen asked.

"Maybe later. I will have a cup of tea, however," Malachi replied before grabbing the pitcher and pouring himself a glass.

Celestine glanced over at her father, looking for any indication of where the meeting was headed. She watched as he reached into his pocket and pulled out the two journals. He placed them on the table before him, keeping them away from the food and drinks.

The energy in the room shifted when Malachi caught sight of them. He sat his cup down, the sound echoing in the awkward silence. Celestine looked between Malachi and her father, waiting for someone else to make the first move.

"We had the royal scholars compare the handwriting in the journals to known writing samples from King Nicodemus the Second. Once they were satisfied, we placed the book in front of the Mirror of Everlasting Truth, then had the strongest magician our kingdom has inspect it for signs of magical tampering. All of the tests confirmed that this is the genuine journal of King Nicodemus the Second. Furthermore, the information contained within was sufficient to confirm your story, Malachi."

"Wonderful!" Celestine exclaimed.

"I am turning the matter over to Princess Celestine. She will be in charge of determining your position in the kingdom, and you will respect her as the next queen of Yulia," Her father continued.

"Yes, sir. I appreciate your kindness and look forward to serving this kingdom once again," Malachi replied.

When he spoke, tears were forming in the corner of his eyes, but his ever-present smile didn't falter. Celestine only noticed because she was hyper-focused on his every move.

"With that cleared, let's enjoy our breakfast. The rest can wait," The King said, putting the journals back in his coat.

It took everything she had to suppress the excited energy Celestine was feeling. What a moment! She was nearly vibrating with excitement, but knowing that would be silly for a princess, she forced herself to sit still.

"Thank you, Your Majesty, but I'd like to get a head start on my preparations to teach Celestine, so if you would excuse me," Malachi said, standing and bowing.

"Wait, take some with you at least," The queen stopped him.

He turned back, glancing down at all the options. After thinking it over, he snapped his fingers, and a few items disappeared from the table.

"Thank you," He added on his way out.

Celestine waved goodbye, which he returned with a grin. The soldiers standing guard outside stepped aside to let him leave. This time, no one followed him. With him out of the room, she turned back to look at her parents, shocked by the dark look on her father's face.

Noticing his daughter's gaze, the king turned to her, softening slightly.

"What's wrong?" She asked.

"Celestine, what has Malachi told you regarding his past?"

Her father asked.

"Not much, why?"

"After the royal scholars were through with their assessment of the journals, I went and read them myself. The times of King Nicodemus the First and Second have always been a bit of mystery thanks to missing journals, so I wanted to see for myself and better understand Malachi's motives," He began as he took a sip of his drink. "But I never could have guessed what I would see."

He paused, looking down. Celestine glanced over to her mother, seeing how she, too, looked forlorn. Anxiety bubbled inside her as she wondered what could possibly have both her parents looking so shaken up.

"Malachi probably wanted to spare you from the truth since you're still young. The things I read in that book were horrible. Your mother and I were deeply disturbed," He continued.

Celestine glanced over at her mother. There were tears in the queen's eyes as she looked at her daughter. She tried to smile and comfort her daughter, but she could only half manage. Celestine was shocked. What was in those books?!

"We both love you so much, sweetie. Please, never forget that," Her mother struggled to say.

"I love you too. What is this all about?" Celestine asked.

"Well, for the two of us, the mistreatment of those with magic has always been something we could view at a safe distance. We knew it happened, and remnants of those same issues exist today, but we never had to face them because they only exist in very small pockets in the kingdom. Even though you have magic, we only saw you as our daughter, the princess. Seeing how things were back then frightened us. I mean, if that small group of citizens who still hate magic despite our best efforts were to try to hurt you, we would be beside ourselves. I couldn't protect you by myself, and the thought terrifies me," Her father explained.

A moment of silence passed between them. Now that Celestine understood what they were upset about, she perked up. She had thought of this issue before, and she'd come to terms with it a long time ago.

"I appreciate the sentiment, but we don't have to worry about that. Those ideas are outdated, and our people have a much more positive view of magic now, so I'll be fine."

Even with Celestine's reassurance, the king and queen were nervous, but they didn't push the matter further, returning to their breakfast instead. They didn't want to add unnecessary concerns to her plate, so instead, they supported her as best they could.

When she was finished, Celestine stood and excused herself. Her parents quickly gave their goodbyes before she was out of earshot. The soldiers stepped aside for her and bowed as she passed.

She headed straight to Malachi's room to check on his preparation. Well, that was the excuse she planned to use. In reality, she was just nosey. She hoped to catch him while he was still working. That way, she could offer to help. Speed walking down the hallway, her excitement grew as she got closer.

The first thing she noticed when she got to his hallway was the new door. The night before, when she left, there was just an open door frame like when she first found the room. Where did this one come from? Upon closer inspection, she noticed the wood looked brand new, and the floor was spotless, free from any debris that would have been left behind during installation.

Then, she remembered Malachi mentioning he would make another one after he was cleared of suspicion. Reaching up, she knocked.

"One moment," Malachi called from within.

It wasn't long before the door opened. Standing there with a partially eaten pastry, Malachi looked down at her. He leaned against the door frame, smiling at her.

"Was wondering how long it would take you to come knocking," He laughed.

"Sorry, am I interrupting you?"

"Not at all. I'm almost done prepping for your first lesson if you'd like to come in," Malachi said, turning and heading back inside.

Celestine followed close behind, excitedly looking around the room for hints for today's tasks. She was amazed by how much the room had changed overnight. The furniture and layout of the room were the same, but the decor had changed drastically. Now, all sorts of fantastical objects were lying around, and anything related to his former position as prince had been stripped away. It looked like the lair of an eccentric wizard now.

Celestine sat at the desk, watching as Malachi walked over to the bed and continued his work. Laid out on the comforter were a couple of stones, a book, and a gnarled stick. He picked up a blue stone and quickly stuffed the last of his pastry into his mouth. As he chewed, he pulled a polishing cloth out of his pocket.

Watching closely, Celestine scrutinized every detail. He was just polishing the stone, but she made a note of every little thing, even down to the angle at which he held it. When he stopped to inspect the stone, she watched how he held it up to the light and twisted.

"Tell me, what do you know of stones and magic?" He asked.

"Um, nothing really. The first time I had ever seen magic stones was at Magitrea," She answered.

"Surprising. This is where I suggest magic users start. You see, stones take magic incredibly well."

"Really?"

Malachi set the stone down once he was satisfied. Then he picked up two different stones, one clear and one blue. When he lifted them, she noticed that the clear one was free of imperfections, looking like a piece of glass rather than a natural stone. Meanwhile, the blue one had a couple of cracks and chips.

"Yes, however, not all stones take magic the same way. Things like cracks and imperfections decrease a stone's affinity for magic, and different types of stones behave differently," He paused. "Let's see, imagine for a moment that we can quantify the quality of the magic in a stone using a number between one and ten. A stone with cracks and imperfections will only be able to reach a three at max, while a stone of the same makeup with zero imperfections could attain a seven or eight."

He reached down and grabbed a third stone, this time, a flawless green one.

"Now, two stones with the same level of flawlessness can also differ in potential due to their type. Take the clear stone in my left hand, it is a flawless white diamond, easily capable of reaching a ten. In my right, I have an equally perfect tear of the forest, yet it can only reach a five at most. As of now, I can not explain the reasoning as to why some stones are more powerful than others. It is just something you learn with time," He continued his lesson.

"Do you happen to have a guide I could use?" Celestine asked.

"Yes. I will give you a copy after we've had a few lessons. It'll only really come in handy when you come across unknown crystals. The rest is up to memorization," He explained. "Since most budding magic users don't have access to the higher-quality stones, I'd like to start there and work our way up. If you succeed at enchanting the hard ones, then you can enchant anything."

He paused.

"Apologies, but these first lessons will seem extremely childish. That's because, in magic communities, children are taught magic as soon as they can hold themselves upright. You're unfortunately several years behind."

"Yeah. I've always been a late bloomer. I didn't show the first signs of magic until I was five," Celestine admitted.

"Really? That's not too bad. What was your first manifestation?"

"Well, whenever I cried, something nearby would turn into a frog."

Malachi snorted.

"Wait, wait, turned into?"

"Yes! One time, I cried because I skinned my knee playing kickball, and the ball turned into a frog," Celestine huffed.

"What did you do with the frog?"

"We gave it to one of the other players, and she kept it for a pet."

"That's hilarious. My first manifestation was when I was two. The maid brought me a tray of little cookies, and she only gave me one. Then she watched another cookie float down from the tray and into my tiny little hand. I wish I could remember the scared look on her face," He laughed.

She chuckled, picturing the frightened maid.

Malachi put the clear stone in his pocket, then returned the green and blue to the pile. There were over a dozen colorful rocks laid out, which Celestine studied, wondering what level of affinity they all had.

"It's a beautiful day out. Would you like to move our first lesson outside?" Malachi asked as he began loading the stones in a small bag similar to one used for marbles.

"Sure!" Celestine smiled, jumping up.

After cinching up the bag, he placed it in his pocket. Grabbing the gnarled stick as he passed the bed, he led her out of his room. Now that he was no longer under investigation, he could roam the castle freely. Word spread quickly among the soldiers, so everyone knew not to bother him.

Knowing they would need a good deal of space for today's lesson, Malachi led Celestine out into the oldest of the castle's courtyards. This one was rarely used after the newer ones were built, but the groundskeepers maintained it. The remnants of a couple of old statues stood out in the open expanse, and there were several flowering trees along the edge, giving the courtyard a sense of privacy and plenty of shade.

Beneath one of the larger trees, Malachi stopped and pulled the bag of stones from his pocket. After checking the ground, he bent down and dumped them out like he were bowling them. The stones scattered, catching the sunlight as they rolled. Malachi took a seat once they settled.

"For your first lesson, you will make these stones float," He declared, resting his head on his arm, which he supported with his knee.

Pumped up due to her excitement, Celestine went to try it but realized almost instantly that she still had no idea what she was doing.

"Alright. How do I do that?" She asked.

"Remember the stones back at Magitrea?"

"Yes, sir."

"To make those float, you commanded them to rise. Do the same thing, but with these," Malachi explained as if it were the simplest thing.

Celestine was dumbfounded. That was one of the most unhelpful explanations in the world, and she feared it was the best she would get. Confused, she decided to give it a try anyway.

"R-Rise," She said, unease and confusion evident.

"No, no, no. That wasn't a command. That was hardly a statement. You need to boss these rocks around," Malachi corrected.

She squared her back and adjusted her stance, mustering up as much commanding energy as she could.

"Rise!" She demanded.

The stone she had focused on, a purple one off to the side, remained still. Its shiny surface mocked her.

"See, now you're just yelling. Put your whole body into it," Malachi chuckled.

Celestine sighed, adjusting once again before retrying. Just like before, the stone, as well as all the others surrounding it, stayed still. She hoped she'd get one of the others by chance, but she wasn't so lucky.

She continued trying, making small changes between each attempt. After a few, she added her hand, gesturing upward in the hopes that that would be enough to finally make it work, but to no avail. Off to the side, Malachi watched in amusement. Her growing frustration made for quite the show. When she used both her hands, throwing them up in the air like a madwoman, he could no longer keep his giggles to himself.

"Don't laugh! I'm trying my best," Celestine whined.

"I know, I know," Malachi spoke between fits of laughter. "It's endearing, really. Reminds me of my early days, is all."

"Well, isn't there a way for you to help me besides crummy tips? Failing over and over again is only going to make me miserable."

Knowing she'd made a valid point, Malachi relented, reaching into his pocket and pulling out the gnarled stick he'd had back in his room.

"Here, some magic users perform better when they have an object through which they can 'focus' their magic. I'm not a fan, but maybe you'll have some luck," He said, holding the stick out to her.

She looked the stick up and down, not sure how it could possibly help; however, with how little success she's had, she was willing to try anything. She took the stick from him and turned back to the little purple stone.

In the grimoire her mother had given her, she had read about the use of "wands", which she believed this stick was meant to be, but it was far from the image she had in her head based on descriptions. She gave it an experimental swish, feeling its weight in her hand. It didn't feel like anything beyond a normal stick, but she forced herself to see it as a mystical object filled with power. Maybe one day, she'd get a fancy wand like the ones in her grimoire instead of this rejected piece of kindling.

She aimed the wand at the stone and once again commanded: "rise".

From her position, it looked like nothing happened, so she tossed the wand down in frustration, prompting a yelp from

Malachi.

"Wait! Calm down, you actually did it," He yelled before she could run off in a huff.

"No, I didn't! That stupid rock didn't budge," Celestine groaned.

"Come here, look closely," Malachi said, gesturing for her to bend down.

Rolling her eyes, she did as he said, bending as low as possible without touching the ground. She turned her head, looking at the bottom-most point of the stone, which looked like it was still pressing against the dirt.

"See? Nothing happened."

"No, look. The stone has risen, but only barely. At most, you could probably slip a sheet of paper under there," Malachi explained.

Celestine tilted even further, finally noticing the tiny sliver of space below the rock. It was pathetic, almost worse than if it hadn't moved at all.

"Now you know that you *can* move something with your magic, and even though it's not by much, you'll only get better. All it takes is building up your strength through practice," Malachi encouraged.

The princess huffed, throwing her arms to the side. The rock dropped when she did, having been released from her influence. She plopped down beside Malachi, scooting close to the tree to enjoy its shade. It was embarrassing to struggle so much and lift the stone an imperceptible amount, but she was looking at it the wrong way: physical strength and strength in magic couldn't be more different.

Glancing over, Malachi gave her a knowing smile, remembering when he, too, grew frustrated with his own inability. It had to be even worse for her, considering she wasn't a child but was struggling worse than one.

"Let's take a break. We can relax in the library for a minute," He offered.

"Alright, and while we sit, I'd like to discuss our game plan for your new job," She replied.

Malachi nodded and stood, helping her up. After gathering their supplies, the two headed off toward the library.

"Am I doing good?" She asked, eyes bright.

"Oh? Weren't you two seconds from quitting just a moment ago?" Malachi teased.

"Eh, the heat was getting to me, but seriously, am I doing good?"

Malachi paused, pretending to be thinking really hard.

"Hey!" Celestine whined.

"Just kidding. You're doing just fine, Princess. 'Progress is progress', I always say," He replied.

"So, for a first-timer, I did alright?" Celestine fished for a compliment.

"If I say yes, will you stop asking?"

Celestine glared at him, then rolled her eyes, grinning to herself. Malachi smiled when he saw her grin. It reassured him that she was serious about this and wouldn't let a little setback stop her.

Chapter 11

Malachi's lessons for Celestine didn't always make sense to her, but every day, she gave one hundred and ten percent. Even when she was exhausted from handling her political duties, she worked as hard as possible. For her, the worst part wasn't the physical toll but how slowly she was progressing.

She didn't care that she had to work hard. She was prepared to do that from the start, but spending every day busting her hump with nothing to show for it, was starting to wear on her. Malachi was always kind and encouraging, but none of his words made her feel better.

"I am going to grind these stupid rocks into powder to spread them like ashes!" She groaned, letting the three stones she had raised five inches fall to the ground.

Hearing the clattering sound, Malachi opened his eyes and glanced at her. He'd been lounging against a tree nearby, letting her do her own thing now that she was getting the hang of it.

"That wouldn't do you any good," He reminded her.

"I know, but it would be so satisfying," Celestine said, plopping beside him under the tree.

She leaned her head against the trunk, relaxing for the first time that day. For the past week, she'd been making preparations to travel to Viridisia for the magic exhibition. Their queen had been incredibly kind in the letters the two had exchanged after she decided she was going to participate, but Celestine couldn't help being intimidated by her.

She was five years older and already the sovereign leader. From what she had read, the queen was praised by her people as one of the most refined rulers they'd had in a long time. How was she supposed to compete with that?

"Would you like to take a break?" Malachi asked.

"Sure. I need to speak with you about the exhibition anyway," Celestine said, sitting up to look at him.

"Alright. What do we need to talk about?

Quickly, she ran through all the speaking points she remembered earlier, organizing them in her head so she wouldn't forget anything.

"The queen of Viridisia sent me a rough outline of what to expect for the competition since it's our kingdom's first time entering. I thought we could sit and run through it, maybe plan out your performance," She explained.

"Nah. I want it to be a surprise. Spontaneity can work in my favor and force me to get creative," Malachi laughed.

"But you need to plan! What if they ask you for something you can't do?"

"There's *nothing* I can't do," He reassured her.

"I appreciate the confidence, but I don't know if we can succeed just by winging it this time."

Standing up, Malachi collected the stones she'd been practicing on earlier. He pulled out and opened the bag he stored them in, then commanded them to return.

"Hey, do we have a plan for our gift?" He asked.

"W-What gift?" Celestine asked, standing up.

"You know. Whenever you visit another kingdom, you bring a gift. Yulia has never had a relationship with Viridisia, so it's important that we make a good first impression."

Celestine froze. All the other times she visited other kingdoms, her parents handled all the social responsibilities, so she hadn't learned them yet. She watched how her parents acted, but the things they did never really stuck in her mind.

They barely had over a week until the exhibition. How was she supposed to get an extravagant present together in time? Tons of ideas popped up in her head, but none were good enough. She knew some amazing artisans that could make a gift, but there wasn't enough time.

Noticing the look on her face, Malachi smiled, placing his hand on her shoulder reassuringly.

"Don't freak out, kiddo. I'll handle the gift. You just focus on making preparations for travel and stuff like that, okay?"

"Alright, I can do that," She replied, calming down slightly.

"We're going to need some security for the trip. Do you have any ideas for that?" He asked, taking her mind off it.

"Yes. I figured we would travel light as a show of trust. At most, I was thinking two attendants."

"Alright, that sounds good to me. We should be fine if we are as discreet as you were when you visited Magitrea."

Celestine didn't mention who she had in mind, but Malachi had a good guess.

"That's the plan. I've already arranged for a carriage to be prepared. I'm working on planning my outfits now," She continued.

"I can't help you with that one," He paused. "That reminds me, I need to start planning my own. I might need to have something tailored. On that note, do you have any reports on Viridisia I can read?"

"Yes, there's a few in the second-floor library."

"Thanks, I'll go check them out. They might help get some ideas for a gift or the best clothes to wear," Malachi said, turning to check them out and leaving her to deal with whatever she needed to get done.

Things got busy during the days leading up to the exhibition, so magic lessons had to be put on hold. The two communicated briefly whenever they could, and occasionally, Celestine had letters taken to him when she was too busy to go in person. As soon as she had time, she asked Vivian and Auberon to join the trip, which they gladly accepted, so everything was lined up.

When they were to leave, Celestine got up early to get ready. Then she took her luggage down to the side of the castle where they planned to meet. When she got there, she found Vivian and Auberon prepping the horses.

Just like on their trip to Magitrea, their carriage was free of any identifying markings or needless embellishments. It was a simple vehicle, not dissimilar from the ones used to transport goods to markets and far from the flashy ones royals always took.

"Good morning, Princess," The two greeted, pausing their activities and bowing.

"Good morning, you two," She replied, taking her bags to the back.

Vivian straightened up and took her luggage, adding it to what was already stacked in the back. Celestine thanked her and walked to the front to check on Auberon. She found him hooking up the horses and ensuring the equipment was steady for the journey. Before they left, she wanted to have a conversation with the two of them, but before she could, Malachi approached.

"Good morning, everyone!" He called out excitedly.

He was extremely chipper, swinging his bag by his side. He handed Vivian his bag, then walked over to join Celestine and Auberon at the front.

"Is everything ready for us to go?" He asked, reaching out and petting the nearest horse.

With his free hand, he made a waving motion, and a long orange carrot appeared in his grasp, which he happily fed to the horse.

"Almost. Once Vivian ensures everything is secured, we can leave," Replied Auberon.

"We're good to go!" Vivian called as she approached from behind.

"Alright, load up, everyone," Auberon nodded and gestured for everyone to hop in.

They agreed beforehand that Vivian should remain inside the carriage while Auberon drove. That way, the carriage looked even more unassuming. Very few would rob a plain-looking vehicle that wasn't even important enough to guard.

It was spacious enough for the three of them to sit comfortably without pressing together. Vivian sat beside Celestine, and Malachi sat facing them. Vivian tapped the wall when they had settled in, letting Auberon know they were ready to go. With a flick of the reigns, the group was off.

Viridisia was less than a week's trip from Yulia: lucky for them. The queen was gracious enough to let the four of them stay a few nights for the exhibition if they would like. They planned to stay a little extra for some friendly political discussion before heading back. Opportunities like this have to be fully exploited.

None of them had been to Viridisia before since the two kingdoms carried out all their correspondence either through letters or at other political functions. Still, they all did their research to prepare themselves. During the ride, they discussed what they had learned as well as how they planned to compose themselves during their visit.

According to the books they read, the citizens of Viridisia were the descendants of flower spirits that settled below a mountain range beside a large river that fed into the ocean. Their main exports were fine silk fabrics and various crops grown on their river banks. Due to their flower spirit ancestry, a hierarchy developed that was dependent on how human each citizen appeared. Those who were more flower than human were typically considered lower class, while those with minimal flower features were revered.

"This is going to sound so terrible of me, but is there a foolproof way to tell if a flower is a person or just a flower?" Vivian asked.

"Not going to lie, I had that same concern. I was so scared I'd greet someone only to find out it's just an extremely large sunflower," Malachi laughed.

"From what I read, that used to be a problem, but the citizens have grown more and more human with each passing generation, so it's no longer an issue," Celestine explained, having had similar concerns before.

"Thank goodness. I think I would die of shame if I made that mistake." Vivian shifted to look out the window and scan the area.

"Don't worry, I'm pretty sure that, of the four of us, I'd be the one to make a fool of themselves," Celestine reassured her.

The four of them talked for the majority of the carriage ride. Whenever Auberon wanted to join in on the conversation, he reached back and opened the partition so they could hear him clearly. When they ran out of things to talk about, they would either take naps or play road trip games. Celestine brought a couple of books and offered one to Vivian, but she declined, saying she needed to keep an eye out for anything suspicious.

On the final day of their journey, they woke up excitedly, ready for the trip to be over. It was well after sundown when Auberon called out to let them know they were approaching the outskirts of Viridisia. They sat up slowly, their bodies stiff from the ride, and leaned toward the windows to view the city. It was dark, but in the distance, they could see lights.

The wilderness was slowly broken up by signs of civilization the closer they got. Stone lanterns lined the road, their lights shining a vibrant crimson. Upon closer inspection, the group noticed that the flames inside were shaped like a flower that slowly spun in place. They bathed the path in brilliant red, not so bright as to hurt the eyes but just enough to light the way.

They didn't see any people until they reached a bridge that crossed a waterway and marked the city limit. To the side, a man was sitting on a box and fishing. Hearing the approaching carriage, he turned, letting the group look at the countless flower petals covering his head. They started just above the midpoint of his nose and completely consumed the upper portion of his face, but he still had a fully formed mouth and chin.

When he raised his hand to wave, they could see root-like

structures running through the skin on his palm and the exposed portion of his arm. He went back to his fishing as soon as they passed.

"How much farther to the castle?" Celestine.

"Another fifteen sexigisms, Princess," Auberon replied.

The trio inside the carriage looked with wide eyes out the windows, taking in as much of their surroundings as possible. Everything was so different from what they were used to back home. The streets were lined with two-story buildings with tall roofs with upward-curving edges. The first floors of these buildings mostly consisted of restaurants or stores, while the second were residential. Some nicer buildings had balconies where the occupants kept plants or hung laundry out to dry. Rather than doors, the entrances to many were covered by noren with brilliant flower patterns and characters written on them that the group couldn't decipher. Occasionally, there were symbols that the group recognized, such as the image of a fish on a building that smelled like a fish market, but other than that, their only clues to what the buildings contained were the glimpses inside they managed to catch or the sight of people carrying things as they exited.

"Wow," Vivian gasped as she caught sight of a trio of citizens walking in the street.

These three appeared to be more flowers than humans, like plants parading as people. There were large blossoms where their heads should be, and their limbs looked like they were made from flower stems. It reminded Celestine of what a child would make if they wanted a doll but only had flowers to work with. The trio looked up at them as they passed, their featureless faces staring blankly up at them. They wore drab yukata and carried toolboxes, suggesting they might be mid to lower-class.

They only saw a handful of citizens the rest of the way, but they could hear the sounds of rowdy late-night crowds inside the various restaurants and food stalls. Seems Viridisia has a thriving nightlife that none of them had heard of during their research.

Once they got close, they could see just how massive the castle actually was. It towered above every other building and spanned several blocks. To the right of the main building, a beautiful pagoda sat on the castle grounds, illuminated by countless lanterns shining with red light. It towered above the city like a watchtower, with an elegant beauty befitting a castle.

"We're almost there, everyone," Auberon announced, although they had noticed by now.

"The queen said someone should be waiting for us at the gate. Do you see anything yet?" Celestine asked, sticking her head out the window.

"I think I see something."

Celestine leaned further out, looking for the castle gate. It took a moment of scanning before she found it: a beautiful, flower-shaped opening in the wall surrounding the grounds where two armed guards stood. In the center of the opening stood a young woman wearing a billowing blue and white hanfu that fluttered around her in the gentle evening breeze. The woman was looking around, checking the streets, so they assumed she was the person the queen had sent to greet them.

Once the carriage was a few yards away, the guards tensed up, angling the spears they held toward the approaching strangers. The woman in the center stepped forward, looking down at them with scrutiny.

A safe distance away, the carriage came to a stop.

"State your business," She commanded, her voice cutting

across the space between.

"Visitors from Yulia m'lady," Auberon called back as he stood and bowed.

The woman raised her hand, and the guards returned to their resting position. She then walked toward the carriage. Her expression was softer but still held a twinge of scrutiny.

"Welcome to Viridisia. You may all exit and follow me. We have prepared accommodations for the four of you," She said in a very flat, practiced tone.

The trio inside nodded, getting up and exiting before grabbing their things from the back. Vivian and Auberon handed Malachi and Celestine their things before grabbing their own. Once they had distributed all the luggage, they turned back to the woman and noticed that a few attendants had arrived.

They looked much like the people they had seen on the streets on the way here, with excessive flower features that replaced or overcrowded some of their human features. The attendants bowed to the four of them before starting their respective tasks. Two of them took the horses' reins and guided them off toward the castle's stables, while another two offered to carry the group's luggage.

"Oh please, don't trouble yourselves," Malachi held up a hand to stop them.

Vivian did the same, but seeing how disappointed they looked, Celestine allowed them to take her things. The ones with mouths gave her bright smiles in return, and then they walked off, taking their things to the rooms they would be staying in. The woman from before stepped in front of them.

"Allow me to introduce myself. I am Meiying Pan, Viridisia's state magician."

"It is a pleasure to meet you," Celestine said, followed by a similar greeting from Malachi.

At first glance, she looked like a beautiful young woman with a round face dotted with pinkish little freckles, but now they noticed that what they thought were freckles were actually small pink flowers. Countless tiny blossoms dotted her face, and they could see a couple of blossoms along the exposed portion of her shoulders.

"The queen sends her deepest apologies. Preparations for tomorrow's tournament have been more demanding than she expected, and she won't be able to greet you until afterward. She hopes you rest well tonight and looks forward to treating you to a private tour of the city," Meiying explained.

"No worries. We completely understand," Celestine replied as Meiying led them inside.

Two attendants fell in line behind her. They were stockier than those who had taken their luggage.

As they passed through the gate, they entered a beautiful courtyard dotted with elegant trees and sophisticated stone statues. A stream that fed into a small pond provided a pleasant trickling sound as well as added to the overall ambiance. They quickly glanced over the edge and noticed beautiful fish swimming through the water.

Exiting the courtyard, they were led through a maze of twisting hallways full of people scrambling to complete preparations for tomorrow. They paused to bow when they saw the group before returning to their frantic duties. They stopped in a hallway filled with doors and decorated with incredible flower and animal designs on the shoji walls.

"The rooms are all the same, so please choose whichever you would like. With how many guests we are receiving, we've had to resort to more quaint accommodations. We hope that you can forgive this oversight on our part," Meiying said, bowing in shame.

"No troubles. We completely understand and are grateful for what you've been able to provide," Celestine was the only one important enough to answer on their behalf.

"Thank you. Please enjoy your rest tonight, and I look forward to competing with you tomorrow," Meiying said, straightening up and leaving.

The attendants following behind them left with her, leaving them alone in the hallway. After saying sufficient goodbyes, everyone turned and picked one of the available rooms. Celestine's bags were sitting beside the door of one of the rooms on the right, so she went with that one while the others chose from the remaining three.

They were a bit different from what they were used to, but the castle attendants had done everything they could to ensure their visitors would be comfortable. There was minimal furniture, and what was there was more in line with what the people of Viridisia would be used to, so they worried they wouldn't be able to adjust. Thankfully, they wouldn't be there long enough for that to become a problem.

On the table in the center of each room, which was much shorter than any table they had ever seen before, was a bowl of perfectly ripe fruit with a card. The card thanked them for visiting and had a short paragraph detailing the economic and cultural status of the kingdom, inviting them to attend their plays and opera concerts or to try on their silks before they leave. After giving the card a read and enjoying a piece of fruit or two, the four went to sleep.

The next morning, attendants came to their rooms to retrieve them for the competition's opening ceremony. Breakfast would be served afterward, so they only needed to get dressed and grab anything they could possibly need to compete. When she was ready, Celestine waited in the hallway for the rest of her group, not wanting to leave anyone behind, which the servants didn't mind.

The first to join them was Auberon, who wore a perfectly pressed suit and carried a notebook to make annotations with. Vivian was next, wearing a lovely suit of armor and carrying her sword at her hip. Moments later, Malachi followed behind, dressed in an outfit similar to the hooded robe he wore back in Magitrea but with a touch more dignity.

"Well, don't you look like the perfect magician," Celestine joked.

"Don't I? I thought the robe added a bit of mystery," He replied, posing with a finger on his chin and looking off into the distance in contemplation.

Celestine laughed, and Malachi grinned. He walked over and took his place beside her, ready to go. They were then led to the ceremony hall.

The kingdom had gone all out decorating the ceremony hall for the exhibition. There were countless fresh flowers arranged in intricate patterns along every available surface. The ceremony hall was two stories, and on the second floor, a large crowd of nobility from all over had gathered to watch. As the members from the participating kingdoms filed in, they began to whisper among each other.

"Quite a crowd," Malachi whispered, noticing how nervous Celestine had become in the face of such a large group.

"Oh yes. I'm shocked."

"Me too. I don't even recognize some of these nations."

Malachi looked around, checking for symbols or flags to identify which kingdom the people were from.

Some wore their nation's colors or had their royal crest emblazoned on a piece of clothing in order to forgo the more flashy flags. As he looked, he went from just glancing to actively searching.

At the head of the room, a temporary platform had been set up with the throne at its center. Meiying stood to the throne's side, watching everyone moving about the room. Her eyes never rested on one point for very long. Behind her, a woman in a massive, dramatic hanfu, walked up the stairs. Meiying turned to her and bowed, followed by the rest of the staff.

The entire room got the hint and prostrated themselves before the queen of Viridisia. No one straightened up until she had taken her seat.

Queen Hualing Lian of Viridisia was considered one of the most perfect members of her kind, with minimal signs of her flower spirit heritage. At first glance, it was impossible to tell she was anything other than human. She had long, black hair that was pulled up very simply with an obscene amount of jeweled accessories for the ceremony. Her skin was free of all marks or blemishes, and the bright red lipstick she wore made each of her lips look like delicate flower petals. The only abnormality on her body was her eyes. Two bright pink irises gazed at the crowd, in their center, light pink, flower-shaped pupils silently scrutinized every single attendee.

Satisfied, she initiated the ceremony with a wave of her hand.

Chapter 12

The opening ceremony was ridiculously flashy. Viridisia put an insane amount of resources and energy into the performance as it was their main chance to show off. They were the hosts of the competition, and while members of royalty from other kingdoms were there, they wanted to show them what they had to offer. It was performative advertising.

Focusing on one thing for a long time was bound to make you sick, so you had to take the entire thing in all at once. The crowd watched as people did tricks, lit fireworks, and twirled ribbons or fabrics.

It was unlike anything they had back in Yulia. The closest thing they had were the occasionally traveling circuses but even those paled in comparison. During the more exciting moments, Celestine would grab Vivian or Auberon's hands in shock.

Malachi was not as impressed as the others, thanks to all the time he had lived in Magitrea. There were countless people who chose to busk on the streets using their magical talents, so he had seen a variety of harrowing performances.

When the performance concluded, the hall filled with excited applause. The performers gave a humble bow before exiting in their performance groups. The more outgoing of the bunch blew kisses or waved to the crowd as they went, bathing in their praise.

A group of Viridisian citizens dressed in all black then scampered across the stage, clearing out the remnants of the last performance and replacing them with large, hand made structures. The crowd watched curiously as the stagehands transformed the scene into a mountain basin complete with lush groves of trees and a flowing river made from several layers of blue silk that stagehands shook to mimic the appearance of water.

Once everything was in place, soft, string instrumentals filled the hall from somewhere unseen, and then a group of citizens stepped onto the stage. They were all mostly humanoid, but they wore costumes that made them appear even more flower-like. Swaying along to the music, they walked through the mountain basin, looking all around as though lost.

Celestine was unsure what was being portrayed, and Auberon noticed the perplexed look on her face.

"I believe this play is depicting the founding of Viridisia," He whispered.

"Oh! I read a retelling of the story while researching, but I bet this will be more exciting," She replied.

The flower people approached the edge of the "water," and the leader peered over the edge. They turned back to the others and smiled, pointing to the water and surrounding area, a silent sign of approval for the location.

Celestine recalled how the story claimed the flower spirits Viridisian's were descended from had traveled for months before they arrived at the river. Human loggers had destroyed their previous home. She mentally rejoiced when she read the humans weren't from Yulia.

Suddenly, the music crescendoed and increased in tempo. From the corner of the stage, a loud drum beat like a growling animal sounded out. The flower people huddled together for safety as a massive river serpent made of dowels, fine silk, and other decorative pieces that jingled as it moved. A group of people controlled the serpent puppet with long sticks, making it fly around gracefully and open its mouth to "roar' at the crowd. The gathered royals gasped and cheered but were barely audible over the high-tempo instrumentals.

The serpent surrounded the performers, flying around them in predatory circles. This was the serpent's river, and it wouldn't let the intruders take its territory. A flower spirit dressed in pure white robes stepped out of the protective huddle. His head was covered from the nose up with petals like those on a lotus flower. He wasn't one of the original actors who stepped out onto the stage, giving the illusion that he appeared out of nowhere.

Seeing the bold newcomer, the serpent dove forward with its mouth wide open to swallow the foolish challenger, but the man did not flinch. He calmly raised his right hand, fingers spread, and waited. The serpent went to swallow the man as the music swelled, but it froze as soon as it made contact with the outstretched hand.

Everything went silent, and the lights in the room went dim. The crowd watched excitedly as a light appeared inside the serpent's belly. Small at first, the light grew, then burst from inside the puppet, scattering little flower petals across the stage. The music and lights returned, celebrating the serpent's defeat as the crowd of actors bowed to their white-clothed savior.

Roaring applause filled the room as the actors bowed proudly. Behind them, stagehands ran around, taking down the structures and cleaning the petals. Once they were done, the actors quickly excused themselves, bowing and blowing kisses even as they went.

As the last one exited, Meiying approached the front of the stage from her place beside the queen.

"Refreshments will now be served in the east courtyard, so you may all go at your leisure. The queen, in the meantime, will be granting audience to any and all guests. Please form an orderly line, as all who desire her attention will receive it," She detailed.

Quickly, the gathered crowd went their separate ways as they chose one of the two options. The queue to speak to the queen grew quickly. Celestine had to rush to get a place in line, dragging her party along with her. Malachi stood by her side while Auberon and Vivian stayed just behind them.

"So what are you going to give her?" Celestine asked.

"It's a surprise," Malachi replied with a grin.

Celestine looked down, noticing he didn't have anything in his hands, nor could she see anything noticeable under his coat. Was the gift really that small that it could fit in his pocket?

"Ah, come on. Can't I get a hint?" Celestine asked as they moved forward in the line.

"I'll give you a sneak peek, but that's it," He laughed.

He reached into his coat and pulled out a shallow, rectangular box. The outside was painted bright gold and wrapped with a red silk ribbon.

"That tells me nothing," Celestine sighed.

"Ah, just trust me. I put a lot of thought into this one," Malachi assured her as he slid it back in place.

Rolling her eyes, she decided to leave it at that. The group had to wait another thirty minutes for their turn, so she looked out at the crowd in the meantime. Once they had their turn with the queen, the royals turned and headed out to join the others in the courtyard. She watched them leave, curious about what they had said.

When their time came, Celestine led the way, cautiously approaching the stage where Meiying and Queen Hualing stood looking down on her. She took a deep breath and began her introduction, speaking more to the crowd than Hualing.

"Thank you for your attention today, Your Majesty. I am Princess Celestine of Yulia, future queen of my kingdom," She paused to wet her lips. "I know our kingdoms have had a... turbulent relationship in the distant past, for lack of a better word, but I am here today to try to change that. My royal magician has prepared a present for you to symbolize our goodwill. I hope it pleases you."

She stepped aside and allowed Malachi to take over, who stepped forward with a flourish. He pulled the box dramatically from his coat, holding it high so everyone could see the beautiful gold exterior.

By now, most people still inside the ceremony hall were watching. Everyone knew Yulia's past with magic, and even though the kingdom had never taken direct action against Viridisia, there was still a great deal of assumed animosity.

Malachi walked slowly up to the platform's edge, holding the box out for Meiying to inspect. After checking with the queen, she bent over and took it. She held her hand above the lid, and her fingertips began to glow a light pink. Pleased with the result, she lowered her hand and brought the gift to the queen.

The audience sat on the edge of their seat, excited to see what the royal magician of Yulia had deemed worthy of smoothing over centuries of bigotry. Hualing removed the ribbon and lid, then reached inside to remove the contents. She lifted it up, revealing a long, beautiful cheongsam to the crowd.

"I hope you like it, Your Majesty. I placed a powerful enchantment on it, one that protects the fabric from any damage. It will never rip or tear, and as long as you wear it, no swords will bring you harm," Malachi explained to her and the crowd.

Gasps filled the room as Hualing admired the gown, inspecting the intricate floral pattern and fine stitch work. Some began to whisper, questioning if the enchantment was really as powerful as Malachi claimed. Others questioned Yulia's motives. When Hualing was finished looking, she folded the gown and placed it back in the box. She then stood and approached the edge of the platform.

"Let it be known today," She began, addressing the room. "That the kingdom of Viridisia feels no animosity toward the kingdom of Yulia. The problems of our past will remain in the past. I hope you all enjoy your time here, and I look forward to collaborating with you in the future."

The end of her speech was aimed directly at the travelers from Yulia. Her glowing flower pupils looked down directly at them, but her gaze was full of kindness.

Celestine finally let herself breathe.

Hualing turned back and returned to her throne as Celestine and her gang were politely ushered aside, and the next group took their place. The princess was covered in goosebumps, and her gait was unsteady as they were led to the courtyard. She didn't speak until the attendants directing them left.

"That was amazing!" She cheered, grabbing Malachi by the arm.

"Yeah! The whole crowd was in awe as we walked out. Their mouths were wide open, " Auberon added, giving him a friendly bump on the arm.

"How did you know what to get?" Celestine asked.

A new attendant walked up to them and led them to a table where they would be served breakfast. Malachi waited to reply until they were seated.

"Well, while I was doing my research, I remembered that there used to be a clothing store in Magitrea that a woman ran from Viridisia, so I popped in for a quick visit."

The attendants brought them plates piled high with a little bit of everything. They recognized some of it, but several dishes were unique to the local area, with the goal of treating them to a presentation of flavors that you couldn't get anywhere else. It was all irresistible, and they quickly started chowing down.

"So the lady showed you what to get?" Vivian asked through a mouthful of food.

"Kind of. She explained the history behind different articles of clothing in her culture, as well as the significance of each one. I got an entire history lesson before I finally bought that dress. Then I took it back and did some tweaking to make it truly spectacular," He explained.

As they ate, Celestine pressed him for more details behind the enchantments. She wanted to know exactly how he did it and what she would need to replicate it. Having a garment that no sword could damage sounded incredibly useful, and she wanted to be the one to make it.

"Well, it's a little beyond your skill set at the moment, but if you want, I can tailor your lessons toward enchantments,"

Malachi explained.

"I don't know. I'd kind of like to be a well-rounded magician rather than a specialist. Besides, shouldn't I follow the order most magicians use to build myself up?" Celestine wondered aloud.

"That is true. Enchantments are a give-and-take form of magic. Usually, they take your energy, making you feel run-down and tired depending on the strength of the enchantment and your strength as a magician. Some require a physical sacrifice and don't take as much of a toll on your body. Either way, a budding magician typically wouldn't be able to handle it," Malachi explained.

"Alright. Let's just stick with the plan for now. I'll learn enchantments eventually," Celestine decided.

Malachi nodded and went back to his breakfast.

There was a surprisingly pleasant atmosphere out in the courtyard. Once they finished eating, some of the political figures walked around and made small talk with the other gathered members of royalty. It was easy to tell which kingdoms were considered the most important by looking at how many people were gathered around their table.

No one walked up to Celestine's group, which was under-standable. Everyone gathered there today was either descended from victims themselves or knew someone who had fallen victim to Yulia's anti-magic tyranny. Yet, there they were like a fox sitting in a hen house with feathers still stuck in its teeth. Any hopes she had of networking were quickly squashed.

Every sideways glare in their direction, they met with an unbothered glance.

"Relax, Your Highness. Your anxiety could be misconstrued as guilt, like you're trying to run from what your family did rather than trying to make it right," Auberon warned her.

"I-I know, but I'm so nervous. Their stares make me feel so small."

Auberon wanted to keep reassuring her, but someone approached her from behind, blocking the sun and alerting her of their presence.

"Good afternoon, Princess," The man in the middle of the approaching trio greeted.

Everyone at the table turned to the visitors. Two men and one woman stood before them. They wore long, heavy cloaks atop finely pressed dress clothes. The man in the center had the finest, most extravagant outfit, with countless accessories and bangles. On his head, he wore a small, simple crown that royalty wear when they go out. To his right, a man wearing a hooded robe stood, staring her down, and on his left, a woman in a modest dress waited patiently.

Celestine recognized them as being from the kingdom of Crescendia, a coastal kingdom several hundred miles from Yulia. The two kingdoms had rarely interacted in the past due to the distance between them, but she had heard that, at times, they quietly supported Yulia's genocide.

"Good afternoon," Celestine replied, standing to shake his hand.

The man stood still, briefly looking at her outstretched hand before resuming staring down at her. His hand never moved: he had no intention of shaking her hand. He had a predatory grin on his face, one that made her skin crawl.

"I'm surprised to see Yulian royalty here, given your history," He said, driving home exactly why he was there.

Hearing what he said, a few patrons seated at nearby tables turned to watch. Many had similar thoughts but didn't have the guts to stand up and say it to their faces.

"W-Well, that's precisely why I'm here! I'm trying to change that," Celestine explained.

"Oh? Tell me, are you the one who'll be competing?"

"No, that would be my…. Uncle."

She paused when it came to figuring out what to call Malachi. It was the truth, just not entirely. She was so focused on making sure the gift and Malachi's performance were spectacular that she had completely forgotten to plan his introduction. She pointed them in his direction, encouraging them to get a good look, but Malachi wasn't just going to let them have an eyeful. He stood, walking over, every step dripping with sass and confidence.

"Charmed. My name is Malachi, and I look forward to competing against whomever you've elected," He introduced himself with a challenging grin.

Unlike Celestine, he didn't even lift his hand for a handshake, like he was too good to be bothered with it. He looked the three of them up and down, surveying them as though they were cuts of meat at a butcher's. This was passive-aggressive revenge for how they had treated Celestine.

"You'll be competing against my champion, Frederick. I'll have you know, he's a master of instrumental magic, known throughout the kingdom of Crescendia as the magician of six strings."

Malachi raised a brow at the king's explanation, looking bored.

"Instrumental magic? I always found that technique lacking, as certain applications never seemed to click. To me, it was restrictive, but everyone finds their niche," He replied with as much malice as he could manage.

The king and his posse were taken aback but quickly bounced back.

"Regardless, the true test will come this evening. We'll get to see if you earned your position through skill or if there was a touch of nepotism at play," The king desperately insulted them, looking toward Celestine.

The curious nobles nearby stifled their gasps.

"We will see. I look forward to it," Malachi said, drawing the king's attention back to him.

The king grimaced. "Indeed we shall."

Without a handshake, the trio turned and left, pretending to be oblivious to the many eyes on them. The onlookers looked away when they met the gazes of those from Yulia. They may not respect them, but they want to at least pretend they do. Malachi and Celestine waited until the trio from Crescendia were long gone before they took their seats.

"How are you feeling, Celestine?" Malachi began.

"I'm alright."

"Are you sure? It's okay to be nervous or frazzled. We're here for you," Vivian spoke up.

Earlier, it took everything she had not to jump up and wedge herself between her princess and the offending trio. Knowing her place, she resisted, only calming down when she saw Malachi going to her aide.

"Yes, I'm fine. Thank you all," She turned to Malachi. "And if you want to make it up to me, kick their asses in the exhibition."

It was another four hours before the attendants came to announce the start of the competition. Once the announcement was made, everyone stood, leaving the food they had been idly nibbling on or the conversation they were in the middle of and heading back inside the banquet hall.

The majority of the decorations and the large platform at the front had been removed. In its place was a long table with five chairs. At the center of the table, queen Hualing sat, watching the participants file in. There were four others at the table that Celestine did not recognize. Their clothing differed from each other, meaning they were all from different kingdoms and allowed for impartial judging.

Those who were not actively participating or representing were asked to sit either on the second-floor balcony or off to the side, away from the main dance floor where the competition was going to take place. Auberon and Vivian joined those on the main floor after giving Celestine and Malachi a quick pep talk.

In front of the judges' table, six stones of increasing size had been laid out, and beside them stood a man in a fine tuxedo. He was this year's officiant for the competition. Every year, one kingdom was chosen to send someone to run the competition rather than compete. This ensures that Viridisia cannot be accused of meddling with the preceding, and since it is not made public which kingdom has been chosen to send the officiant, no one can attempt to make bribes.

Once the audience had stilled, the man began the introduction. He introduced himself and thanked everyone for coming again, then explained the rules.

"This year's competition will consist of three separate tests. The results of each test will be scored on a scale of one through ten by the judges, and whichever nation has the highest score overall will be declared the winner. Our first test will be a test of might. Using only magic, each magician must lift the heaviest stone of these six that they can manage. You are allowed to lift more than one should the heaviest stone prove too easy for you. I will call each nation up one by one, and the candidate will lift their stone. First up, the kingdom of Nandi."

Despite the large crowd, only ten kingdoms had sent magicians to represent them. The ten of them stood there proudly, looking intently at the stones and judges. The representative from Nandi, a young woman of maybe 24 years old, approached the stones. She wasted no time, raising her right hand and causing the middle stone to rise a solid meter off the ground. A loud thud resonated throughout the room when she allowed it to fall. It had to have been at least 100 pounds, yet she lifted it with ease. Celestine was amazed to see someone so skilled when she struggled to raise stones lifting less than a single pound.

The judges said nothing, and the officiant called for the next representative. Therefore, the audience wasn't going to know the results until the end of the competition, so all they could do now was watch with curiosity and commentate, which they did a lot of.

As soon as a participant finished their attempt, the crowd started to whisper and gossip. Celestine couldn't hear any of them clearly, but she caught snippets here and there. Some were impressed. Others were purely cynical. The occasional "my kingdom could do better" was mixed in.

When it was time for Meiying to go, Celestine and Malachi watched closely, excited to see what she was capable of. Standing with her legs slightly apart, she raised her arms slowly, and the largest and second-largest rocks rose, making the audience gasp in shock. Combined, the two rocks had to weigh close to a ton. It was incredible to witness the power she had at her disposal. Considering the fact that it was harder to divide your attention and lift more than one object, her act was even more impressive. After lowering the rocks, she bowed to the judges and returned to her place among the participants.

Malachi nudged Celestine when Crescendia's magician was called up. The two shared a cheeky look, remembering the altercation from earlier. It wasn't proper to wish for someone else's downfall, but they weren't much for proprietary anyway. They watched the man from earlier approach the stones and pull out a six-stringed lyre. The man paused to pose with the lyre in his left hand and his right raised to the heavens before slamming his arm down to play a note.

He was clearly showing off, and the crowd was eating it up. They gasped in awe as the largest and second-largest stones rose. He kept playing, and the stones remained suspended. Even though Meiying had raised the stones higher, the crowd was cheering louder, likely due to the fact that he had wowed them with his showmanship. To lower the stones, the man began to play slower, gradually decreasing the tempo until they landed and the music stopped. With mad applause in his ear, he returned to his place in line.

"Next up, the kingdom of Yulia," The officiant called.

Celestine's breath caught in her throat, and she turned to Malachi. He gave her a reassuring smile before striding up to the front. All the excitement in the room faded. Silence permeated the air as everyone kept their eyes glued to his back. He maintained a brilliant smile all the way, then paused to bow before the judges up front. Unlike the others, he settled into a relaxed position before them, and then he quickly scanned the stones, taking stock of what he had to work with. Deciding his method, he raised his right hand and snapped.

Instantly, the stones began to rise in order from smallest to largest. The other magicians had only raised them a meter at the max, but Malachi made them rise well above his head, nearly reaching the second floor of the ballroom. The entire audience gasped, including Celestine, who quickly corrected her expression to one of pride. Awe twisted the judges' faces, and their jaws nearly touched the floor. This was far from what they expected from the magic-hating kingdom of Yulia.

After waiting long enough for everyone to get a good look, Malachi snapped again, letting the stones fall to the ground with a loud crash. He bowed to the judges once more, then returned to his place by Celestine. There was no cheering, as everyone was too stunned to even speak.

"U-Up next, we have Mbasu," The officiant called out as soon as he regained his composure.

"How did you do that?" Celestine whispered once everyone's attention had shifted to the next participant.

"I told you before, I've lived a long time and used that time to hone my skills. I'm sure that any of these magicians gathered here could reach my level if they lived to be my age," He whispered back.

The two of them watched as the last participant stepped away, allowing the servants from before to come in and retrieve the stones. They were so heavy that they had to lift them in groups and place them on carts so they could roll them away. The officiant returned to the front when they were clear, ready to announce the next event.

Chapter 13

"The second event will be a test of transfiguration. You will all be assigned a plant that you must then transfigure into a bird. Please line up side by side here in front of me," The officiant commanded

Malachi left Celestine and took his place in the line. He was slightly to the left of the center, putting him in everyone's line of sight.

Back in the crowd, Auberon and Vivian watched curiously. They were amazed by the rock challenge and couldn't wait to see what happened next.

The attendants who dealt with the rocks carried ten platforms they individually placed in front of each participant. Behind them, a second group brought in 10 identical peony plants and set them on the platforms. Each plant was the same size, had the same number of blossoms and flowers, and was in the same pot, so no one could say someone had an unfair advantage.

Once everything was situated, the officiant took his spot in front of everyone and raised his hand to get their attention.

"The only rule is that you must transform the bush into some kind of bird. The size and species are completely up to you. On the count of three, you may all begin. One.... two.... Three!"

The magicians raised their hands or whatever instrument they used and began the process. There were many possible ways for them to pull this off; each one went with whatever method they were most familiar with. For the more inexperienced group, the task was too much, so their plants either didn't change at all or changed only slightly. Transfiguration is one of the hardest feats of magic, after all.

In the end, only six of them were able to pull it off. While most of them had changed the plant into a bird of similar size, such as a chicken or owl, Malachi wanted to show off again. He transformed the plant, which was originally around a foot tall, into a three-foot-tall phoenix with shimmering red feathers. The phoenix looked around, occasionally adjusting its feet on the pedestal to stay comfortable.

Those in the audience who were more familiar with the actual processes behind magic gawked at the bird's behavior. Transforming something into something else is already a huge task, but replicating a living, breathing being is even harder. Usually, if the thing is even alive, it doesn't behave like it should. If you turn a rock into a horse, it usually can't walk since it's never been a horse before. Malachi's phoenix was behaving perfectly, like it had always been one.

The officiant then walked over and visually inspected each bird, looking for any issues or imperfections. He started on the left and worked his way to the other end, stopping in front of Meiying.

"Beautiful work. Your duck is perfect. Just listen to that flawless quack."

The audience listened closely, taking in the tiny noises the duck was making before nodding in approval.

The officiant moved down along the line, making commentary as he went for the entirety of the room. Crescendo's bird was nearly flawless, with only a slight kink in the bird's leg, but the magician next to them had massive issues. When the officiant went to touch their bird, his hand passed right through it. Confused, he reached out again and kept trying to grab it, but instead of feathers, he found leaves.

"Steria, I'm sure you understand that using illusions to fake transfiguration counts as cheating?" He said in an even tone, like a disappointed mother.

The magician put their head down, their face turning red. The crowd began to boo.

"We will have to disqualify you. Please return to your place with your kingdom."

The booing continued as the magician left, and the illusion faded. Celestine had never seen an illusion in person before, so she was impressed. Based on what she read in her books, she thought they would be easier to tell apart from reality, but it totally fooled her. She wondered if it would be easier to identify them with time.

When the officiant got to Malachi, he paused to admire his work. The phoenix looked at him, leaning forward to get a better view. It turned its head left and right, inspecting him in return. To check, the officiant reached out and touched the bird's body.

"Incredible! This phoenix is flawless. The color of the feathers, the texture, the shimmer of its beak, it's all perfect! You managed to create something bigger than your starting point, an incredibly efficient use of material," He praised.

The crowd oohed and awed, clapping politely.

After that, it was hard for the officiant to act impressed. Like seeing a miracle and then clapping when water boils. He went through the others fairly quickly, providing minimal commentary, then returned to the front.

"Good work, everyone. If you would now undo your transformations and return to your places, we will begin preparations for the final round," He said.

The magicians quickly released their spells and then returned to their masters. Malachi released his spell with a snap, then walked back to Celestine. The two waited while the attendants cleared out the platforms and plants and assisted the magicians who couldn't undo their transformations.

Celestine watched closely as the judges whispered amongst themselves. Some had papers they were scribbling on and were comparing notes with the others. They spoke too quietly for her to hear what they were saying, making her nervous. Malachi was doing great, but what if their dislike of her kingdom soured their opinions? They weren't there to win necessarily, and as long as the judges made a fair and honest assessment, she'd be happy, but winning sure would be nice.

This time, the attendants didn't bring anything out for the competitors. Instead, they cleared a large area in front of the judge's table. They had to push the first few rows of the crowd back in order to make enough room. Once satisfied, they notified the officiant, who called out.

"For the final round, each magician has to perform some form of magical feat. The method and subject is entirely up to you. The judges will be ruling based on the skill and power required to pull these off rather than the subject. As I call you up, please stand facing the crowd and perform your trick. First up, Crescendia."

Celestine and Malachi rolled their eyes as the obnoxious magician from before took his place up front. He posed like a rock star on a stage, flashing flirtatious grins to the front rows and waving to everyone else. The crowd ate it up, clapping and cheering excitedly. He raised his lyre and silenced the room.

As he began to run his fingers along the strings, lights began to appear around him. These lights shined in all colors of the rainbow, even with all the candles illuminating the banquet hall. They then began to condense, forming into beautiful flowers. As he played, the flowers floated around him in a fabulous display. Some flowers actively bloomed, their petals stretching with each note. His light show expanded at least five feet from him in all directions, covering a large portion of what would have been the dance floor. The crowd was mesmerized.

Malachi leaned over to Celestine and whispered, "It's pretty, I guess, but isn't he being a little heavy-handed with it?"

"Pardon?"

"Flowers are a central part of Viridisia's culture, so they're nothing new here. It's almost like he's saying, 'I can do flowers better than you,'" Malachi explained.

"Oh, I hadn't thought of it like that," Celestine replied.

"I tell you what, wanna make an impression on some judges? Show them something they're unfamiliar with. That way, they don't know enough about it to judge you harshly," He joked.

Celestine chuckled, and the two went back to watching the light show.

Feeling his performance had gone on long enough, he ceased playing, and the flowers disappeared, much to the disappointment of the gathered audience. Still, they clapped and cheered as he returned to his place.

Meiying was up next, but her performance wasn't nearly as flashy. Standing in front of the judges' table with her face toward the crowd, she raised her arms and transformed into a sweet little blackbird. In this form, she flew in front of one of the judges and grabbed his pen, taking it with her as she whizzed around the ballroom. Since she was holding a pen in her beak, a pen she didn't put a spell on, she could prove it was a transformation, not an illusion. When she was finished, she transformed back and returned the pen before bowing to the crowd.

Shapeshifting is one of the hardest forms of magic out there, and to do it correctly is something only the finest magicians can manage after years of study. It may not have been a flashy performance, but it proved that she was one of the finest magicians living today.

Surprisingly, Malachi was called up last, adding another layer of pressure to his performance.

"Good luck," Celestine whispered.

"Don't worry. I've always said magic is 80 percent showmanship. I've got this," He laughed.

Once again, he strode up to the front of the room, not even acknowledging the eyes on him. After his previous performances, everyone was excited to see what he would come up with. At the front, he paused, making faces as though he was struggling to think of something.

He adjusted his stance and rubbed his chin, making a show out of thinking. Then he lifted his head, giving a "eureka!" face. He spread his feet apart and bent his knees while squaring his shoulders. He raised his hand and tapped on his chest like one would do if they were choking, simultaneously puffing up his cheeks. With each tap, he puffed his cheeks up further and further as though his actions were forcing something out of his body. Once they were full, he raised his hands and balled them into fists. He then placed those fists over his lips, like you would when playing an instrument, and began to blow.

A small shape began to emerge from the hole in the center of the outer fist. A fish swam out of the hole, followed by countless other ocean creatures. They flowed out like bubbles, floating around the room mindlessly. Each creature moved on its own, swimming through the air just like it would in the ocean. He continued blowing until the room was filled with an entire ocean's worth of sea life. The creatures looked like they were made of glowing water, but when the light hit them just right, their features would change, looking more realistic.

The crowd gasped in awe as they watched the creatures swim around them. Children squealed with delight as they reached out to grab the smaller fish nearby. When their fingers grazed them, it felt as though they were touching the real thing. They could even feel each individual scale.

While Celestine stared in awe, a tiny school of fish swam over and started playing in her hair. They swam around her in circles, occasionally darting into her hair, messing it up. She laughed, knowing Malachi was probably doing that on purpose.

A massive whale swam high above the first floor, rising till it nearly touched the ceiling before diving back down with a loud groan, sending a breeze through the crowd.

Malachi released the spell once he felt he had done enough, causing the fish to pop like bubbles and a gentle mist to rain down on the audience. This time, they erupted into applause, jumping to their feet if they were not already standing. It was like they had completely forgotten his heritage. He basked in their praise.

"Thank you all. Viridisia is a landlocked country, so I wanted to bring the ocean to you," He said before walking back to Celestine.

The officiant had to take a moment to recover before making his next announcement.

"Everyone, the judges will now tally up the points. While you wait, we will provide refreshments here in the ballroom and east courtyard."

The judges stood and exited the room as the crowd went their separate ways. Those who were directly involved chose to stay inside, while many of those who were in the audience only chose to step out for some fresh air. Auberon and Vivian worked their way over to Malachi and Celestine, maneuvering through the crowd.

"That was amazing, Malachi!" Vivian praised.

"I had to put my best foot forward," Malachi laughed it off.

Auberon noticed that the people around them were looking at them differently than before. They were still the center of attention, but the glares had disappeared now they looked on respectfully with a touch of apprehension. They were scared to approach, only now it was out of reverence. The rest didn't notice, talking and laughing without a care, so Auberon ignored it.

"How do you think you did?" Vivian asked.

"Well, I don't want to jinx myself, but I'm sure I did fine. I'm the most experienced magician here by far, so if I lose, then it's my own fault," He laughed.

The judges weren't gone for very long. The steady chattering died down when they returned, and the crowd surged to the front. Word reached those outside, and they poured in, squeezing in wherever they could find space.

Every judge except for Queen Hualing took their seat. The queen remained standing, looking at the crowd. She waited silently as those who had been outside finished filtering in. As she heard the door shut, she began her speech.

"Thank you all for coming today. This year was better than we could have ever anticipated, and that was thanks to the amazing audience and participants," She paused as the crowd applauded. "I will now announce this year's top three. Today, we saw magic redefined, making it incredibly difficult to decide on our winners, so all participants should pat themselves on the backs, even if they weren't in the top three. In third place, we have Crescendia."

The group from Crescendia cheered loudly, throwing their arms up and jumping around. At the center, the magician raised his lyre proudly.

"In second, we have Viridisia."

The crowd turned to Meiying, and she bowed professionally in response, waving in a very robotic and practiced fashion. All the servants that had helped out clapped excitedly as well, but nowhere near as crazily as those from Crescendia. When she stood back up, her and the queen made eye contact from across the room, and the queen gave her a warm smile.

"Before I announce first place. I would like to thank everyone once again for coming out."

Celestine grit her teeth as Hualing switched gears and started talking about how nice things had been again.

"For the first time in history, first place in this year's exhibition goes to...... Yulia!" The queen announced, sending the hall into a frenzy.

Those who had gathered today were heavily divided. Some saw this coming and cheered wildly in support. Then there were those who, no matter how skilled Malachi was, refused to celebrate Yulia. They clapped quietly to keep the peace, but the scowls on their faces proved they weren't happy about it. Malachi just smiled and waved to everyone, thanking them.

"The other judges and I will be available the rest of this evening if you would like to discuss ways you could improve for next year. Otherwise, please enjoy your time here in Viridisia, and I look forward to next year's exhibition," The queen announced as the cheers died down, ending the exhibition.

There was no prize, and Malachi didn't see the need to ask for tips, so the four decided to loiter around until the queen was finished. She still owed them a tour, and they planned to cash in on that.

When they stepped outside to get some refreshments, they were bombarded by people. Earlier, no one would come within ten feet of them, but now that Malachi had won, everyone and their uncle wanted a word.

"Where did you learn magic, or are you self-taught?"

"I always heard Yulia is a lovely kingdom. When can I come to visit?"

"Are you a student of Malachi's?"

The four of them were swamped with questions and offers. The surrounding crowd was so dense that they became separated. Vivian, Auberon, and Malachi were totally fine answering questions with poise, but Celestine began to panic.

Surrounded by strangers asking her all sorts of questions and praising her for her skilled magician, it was exactly what she wanted out of this, but now that she was there, her heart sank. It felt like the world was closing in on her. All of their voices ran into each other, turning to static. She looked at Malachi and saw how proud he looked, standing tall among the people, answering questions flawlessly. Why was she struggling so much?

Her mind was swimming, and she could tell her answers were only half coherent when she felt a hand on her arm. Looking up, she saw it was Auberon who met her gaze with a stern yet worried look.

"Pardon me, everyone, but it's time for the princess to practice her daily mantras, can't miss a day. If you would excuse us, I'll bring her right back," He said to the crowd before pulling her away.

He led her to a secluded portion of the courtyard under a massive weeping willow. The branches acted like a curtain, hiding them from the others. After letting her go, he looked around to make sure no one else was nearby before speaking.

"Are you alright? You were freaking out back there."

"No, I'm fine. I had it under control."

Auberon crossed his arms in disbelief, raising a brow.

"Come on, princess. I could see it in your face. You were panicking."

"Okay, maybe a little, but it's nothing I can't handle. I just need to get back out there and face it," She replied, attempting to walk away, but he sidestepped to block her.

"Look, I'm going to let you go back, but I need you to promise me that you're alright and that you won't forget that Vivian and I are there to support you. If you need anything, just get our attention somehow, and we won't hesitate to get you out of there," The look on his face was so serious as he spoke.

He had always been so standoffish. She didn't know he could even show this much expression, let alone look at her with such tenderness. She felt her cheeks lighting up, but she forced herself to calm down.

"I-I promise."

Auberon nodded.

"Alright. I trust you."

He stepped aside and allowed her to return to the crowd. This time, Celestine didn't struggle as much to maintain her composure. Something about being called out made her feel more confident, or maybe it just added a layer of pressure to perform. Either way, she stood tall among the crowd now, answering questions as best she could.

Toward sunset, most of those gathered had either retired to their quarters or headed home, partially clearing out the courtyard. Celestine and her bunch had regrouped and taken a seat over by the waterfall connected to the pond. They relaxed as they listened to the trickle of water and watched the rest of the people chatting.

They hadn't been sitting there long when a small group of people approached. It was queen Hualing, Meiying, and a couple of attendants.

"Sorry to keep you all waiting for so long," Hualing began in lieu of a greeting. "I have finished my duties and am ready for our tour."

The four of them stood.

"Wonderful! We cannot wait to see your beautiful kingdom," Celestine replied.

"If you would follow me, we can begin in the castle."

Hualing led the four of them all around the inner castle as well as the outer walls and courtyards. Despite the fact that she had spent all day running and judging the exhibition, she showed no signs of fatigue. She proudly showed off everything her kingdom had to offer while providing some historical commentary.

Through the tour, they learned a lot about Viridisia's people, which they hadn't found in their textbooks. They learned how the flower spirits their people descended from used to grow massive forests and stay hidden among the treetops, but eventually, they saw the wonders of humanity and the other species that lived on the ground, so they chose to descend. As well as how the royal family led the people across a vast desert to the rich and fertile lands they now inhabit.

According to legend, a great drought centuries ago threatened their people. To survive, they had to leave, but the journey was treacherous. They wandered aimlessly, losing several before the royal family took charge. They used their magic to predict the perils they would encounter and steered the people around them. Then, when they reached the mountain range, they found a beautiful river, which their magic identified as the perfect land to settle on.

"Thank you so much for everything, queen Hualing," Celestine said to her as the sun began to set.

"Think nothing of it. I was excited to see Yulia attempting to make amends and wanted to help as much as I can," She replied nonchalantly

"We're so grateful. Today was a huge step in the right direction for my kingdom. I know we're still a long way from making up for our past, but today gave me hope that we can pull it off."

The two spoke as they walked. The others in their group talked among themselves, asking questions or telling stories, oblivious to their conversation.

"Have you thought of hosting a ball?" The queen asked.

"A ball? Well, we have those sometimes," Celestine replied, not understanding.

"No, no. I mean, have *you,* in particular, thought of hosting a ball? After your performance at the exhibition, all eyes will be on you and your kingdom. Hosting a ball would be a great way to invite everyone in to talk and clear up any misconceptions. It could even open doors for you," The queen explained.

Celestine paused, mulling it over.

"That is true. Now is the perfect time. People are more likely to make amends after a few drinks. Hualing, you're a genius. I mean… queen Hualing," Celestine corrected herself.

The queen laughed. "You'd better save an invitation for me."

Celestine nodded, the gears in her mind already turning.

When the tour was over, and the queen walked them back to their rooms, Celestine was deeply invested in making plans. She was coming up with a guest list, a menu, an entertainment selection, anything that would be necessary to throw a spectacular party. On the way home, she planned to discuss it with the others, not wanting to keep them up. This exhibition proved to be more advantageous than she had originally planned.

Chapter 14

Their goodbyes in the morning were rushed as both parties had work to get back to. The two groups met at the front gate, spoke long enough to get the bare minimum in terms of pleasantries, and then went on their way. For one last going-away present, the attendants from Viridisia loaded a basket full of goodies and placed it inside their carriage to give them something to snack on during the ride home.

They quickly loaded up just like they had on the way there and set off. The four split the food evenly, enjoying it as they rode.

"Alright, everyone, let's have a quick recap session. Who would like to go first," Celestine began.

"I'll go," Auberon said, opening the partition further so they could hear him clearly. "We definitely made some impressive strides this trip. You know, we're not going to undo centuries of violence and hatred in one day, but I think our efforts were well received."

Vivian nodded. "I agree. There was a huge shift in our public image after Malachi's performance, I didn't feel anywhere near the level of malice we received on the first day. Like they were actually appreciating our efforts!"

"I've actually been mulling over a potential public outreach event," Celestine spoke up.

"Really? Do tell," Malachi encouraged.

He was lazily leaning against the carriage wall beside the window, but he sat up when he saw how stoked she seemed.

"Well, I can't take all the credit. Hualing actually suggested that we host a ball back in Yulia to ride the success of the exhibition."

"That's a wonderful idea, princess."

Vivian leaned forward with excitement. She loved the idea and knew it would be great for furthering Celestine's dream of reinventing Yulia.

"Thank you. I did some mental planning last night and have figured out most of it. I'm down to just the guest list and entertainment."

Auberon pipped up. "I can help with that, princess. I've been on plenty of diplomatic trips in my lifetime, so I have a deep understanding of Yulia's standing amongst the other kingdoms, although I think our win at the exhibition may have changed some of that."

"Wonderful. I want my guest list to be strategic. Even including kingdoms that we had bad relationships with in the past."

Malachi raised a brow at her statement.

"Are there any in particular that you had in mind?" Auberon asked.

"Well, for starters, I was thinking Fulminus and Nguromo. We haven't had any issues with them recently, but there was friction in the distant past over their potion and spell industries. Even after Yulia lifted the ban on magic, they remained cold and uncooperative towards us due to our prior behavior toward them. This could be a chance to smooth things over and even open the door for trade," She paused to think of some more. "I think Draconéa would be a major win in our books."

Malachi flinched at the sound, but he twisted it, making it look like the carriage jostled him. The ladies noticed but didn't press the issue, quickly segueing into the next point.

"King Aegis rarely makes an appearance at parties and has outright refused an invitation to any gatherings where Yulia planned to be in attendance for over six hundred years. His distaste for our kingdom is infamous, but maybe the buzz generated by Malachi's win could get his attention."

"Excellent idea, Princess. His visit would send shockwaves across the political sphere. Everyone would want to see the princess who got King Aegis to visit Yulia," Vivian praised.

"What do you think, Malachi?" Celestine asked.

"It's not a bad idea."

His reply was monotone and lifeless. They had never seen him like this before, and it made them uncomfortable. The ladies didn't know what to say next, so they sat, waiting for someone else to speak up.

"Is he still looking for a bride?" He asked, breaking the awkward silence for them.

"Well, that's a complicated question. He's still single, yes, but he turns down any offers for marriage or courtship," Celestine answered.

Malachi paused, reconsidering Celestine's idea.

"Alright. It's worth a shot, I guess. The worst he can do is say no, so we have nothing to lose and everything to gain," Malachi said, finally turning to face the two of them.

"Excellent. I was thinking we could have the party a month from now because of how long it takes for the invites to arrive," Celestine changed the subject, wanting to change the vibes.

"Why wait? I can deliver them instantaneously," Malachi replied.

"Oh! In that case, we can probably do it in 3 weeks or so. It won't take me long to make arrangements, so we'd only have to wait on travel."

For a good portion of the ride, the four planned the party from start to finish. They went over everything from the music down to the color of the napkins they would have. It ended up being a fun conversation, and the four of them often had to pause to laugh as they pictured silly hypothetical situations.

Eventually, they moved on, talking about less important topics and chatting in general. It was a long ride back, so they did whatever they could to pass the time. When they finally made it home, they had exhausted every speaking point they could think of and were in the middle of a carriage ride game.

As Celestine planned, they spent the next few weeks preparing for the ball. Malachi found a way to combine her training with the preparations so she wouldn't have to put those on pause. Malachi made her use magic to move the pen to write her invitation letters. She had already proven she could lift objects, so this was an exercise in movement. Her efforts were incredibly sloppy at first, and most of the letters had to be rewritten, but as time passed, her writing became legible. Then he made her lift and organize the letters with magic, forcing her to make precise movements repeatedly.

Her parents were completely hands-off in the process. As soon as she got back from Viridisia, she met with the two of them to explain her plan and ask for their permission. Based on her pitch, they happily agreed, giving her free rein to do as she pleased. They saw the potential benefits she outlined, but more than that, they trusted her and her judgment when it came to party planning. At most, they were going to make an appearance the night of. Everything else was up to Celestine.

For anyone else, a party of this size would have taken a couple of months to prepare, but for a princess, everything came together. Everyone involved put in double time to make sure they didn't disappoint. She thanked them all profusely for their hard work.

As the party date approached, she was working on figuring out the staffing list when she called Vivian and Auberon for a discussion in her room.

She and Vivian sat on her bed while Auberon stood by the door. They chatted leisurely for a moment before Celestine changed the subject to what she had actually called them in for.

"What do you mean the two of you can't attend?" She questioned.

"Princess, I'll be doing security, so I won't be able to spend time with you," Vivian explained.

"And I'll be busy socializing with the rest of the diplomatic team," Auberon added.

"But I want you two there with me," Celestine whined.

The others shared a glance, making conflicted faces.

"Princess, we are employees of the royal family. It wouldn't be a good look for you to have servants running around your ballroom as guests," Auberon explained to her.

Celestine was taken aback. He was telling the truth, but

it wasn't something that she had considered. To her, their status meant nothing. They were her friends first and foremost. They just happened to also work for her family. She hadn't even considered that their attendance as guests would cause problems.

"But- I- I want you guys to be there with me. I need your support."

"And you'll have it," Vivian scooted closer to her, placing a reassuring hand on top of hers. "We'll just be supporting you from a distance. I'll be at the door, and Auberon will greet guests, so I'm sure you'll see us now and then."

Celestine didn't want to accept that. She wanted, no, she *needed* them to be with her otherwise, she feared she'd panic.

"What if I assign you as my security escort for the evening," She pointed to Vivian. "And have you as my political consultant? I can say I asked you to stay with me and keep me informed." She said to Auberon.

The two considered it.

"If you insist, Princess, I will do it. I just hope you don't receive any negative attention because of me," Auberon answered.

"I agree," Vivian added.

"Then it's settled. I'll ensure your supervisors know about the change, and I look forward to spending time with you two," The princess celebrated.

The three of them continued to chat until they had to return to their duties. They began to grow excited now that they were going to spend the ball with her and talked about how fun it would be.

Once they left, Celestine got up and headed to Malachi's room. With the invitation letters finished, Malachi adjusted her training, having her play a magic game of catch every day for an hour or so. She hadn't gone for today's training, so she headed that way. She knocked on his door to announce her arrival.

"Come in," He called from inside.

She pushed the door open and entered, greeting him as she did but stopping when she caught sight of him. Malachi was sitting on his bed, facing away from the door and surrounded by countless yellowing sheets of paper. He gazed down at the papers longingly, resting his head on his hand. When she walked in, he started gathering them together.

"Sorry, I was reminiscing," Malachi apologized as he stood with the pages and walked over to the hole in the floor.

"No worries. I should be the one apologizing for interrupting you."

She watched as he bent down, put the papers back in the open subfloor, and then returned the board. He stood back up and smiled as though nothing were out of the ordinary, but Celestine noticed how puffy his eyes looked.

"Did I interrupt something? I can always come back," She asked.

"No, no. I'm being sentimental, is all. Here, I've got a five-pound ball for your training today, so let's get started," He replied, pulling the fist-sized ball from his pocket.

She could tell he was hiding something from her, but she wasn't sure how to deal with that. If he didn't want to talk about it, she shouldn't force it, but how could she help him if she didn't know what was happening? Not wanting to stir the pot so close to the party, she chose to leave it.

They began their game of catch like usual. Malachi would toss the ball to her, and she would catch it with magic, then "throw" it back. He then catches it with magic and throws it back. Normally, they chat while they play, but today, he stayed silent. Not sure how to break the silence, Celestine kept her mouth shut.

They went back and forth for one awkward hour before Celestine called it, claiming she had more work to do when, in truth, she just couldn't stand the awkward silence.

"Oh? That's alright. You got your daily hour in, so we can stop," He replied, putting the ball away.

"Yeah, sorry about that. Next week, when all this is over, we can practice longer," She promised.

"Alright. I'll see you later," He said as she walked away.

She stewed over what had happened on the way back to her room. Malachi was acting strange, and she worried it had something to do with the ball coming up. In her opinion, those papers he had looked like letters, but she couldn't tell based on her short sighting. Her detective's brain was running wild with theories. However, she eventually had to conclude that the best way to find out what was going on was to wait.

On the day of the ball, everything came together smoothly. Auberon and Vivian's supervisors were more than happy to give them up for the day if it meant pleasing the princess, so they hovered by her side as soon as she woke up that morning.

Her parents planned to make an appearance at the ball, but they wouldn't stay long. They didn't want anyone to get the wrong idea. This was to be a diplomatic ball hosted by the *Princess* of Yulia.

The guests wouldn't be arriving until that afternoon, but Celestine had an entire day's worth of prep to handle before then. She spoke to Malachi ahead of time and planned to meet him just before the ball began so the two of them, plus Vivian and Auberon, could greet the guests as they arrived. Until then, he was free to do whatever he wanted or needed. He offered to help with the day's prep, but Celestine refused.

The first order of the day consisted of greeting the first group of dignitaries who arrived. Most of the invitees sent back either a polite rejection or an enthusiastic acceptance. Based on those numbers, the castle staff prepped rooms. Since six or so invitations didn't get a response, they readied rooms just in case. Of the confirmed attendants, five chose to consolidate their traveling party into one large caravan, which was arriving early in the morning.

"Do you see them yet, Auberon?" Celestine asked, craning her neck to look for the carriages.

She and her two attendants stood under the Porte cochère, gazing toward the street leading up to it. The main road up to the castle directs any approaching vehicles toward either the Porte cochère or to the front steps, and since the front steps were currently blocked off by castle staff bringing the furnishings into the ballroom, all coaches should head this way.

"Not yet, Princess. Have you practiced your speech for the night?" He asked in return.

"Of course. That speech is going to be burned into my memory forever," She laughed.

Vivian perked up. "I'm sure it's going to be wonderful. Anything you write is sure to be a hit."

Celestine blushed, loving the compliment. She noticed Auberon shift.

"I hear them coming, straighten up everyone," He insisted.

The ladies did as he said, doing their best to stand as straight as possible. It was another few moments before the carriages came into view. Each of them was visually distinct among the group of five. There were markings along the outer walls that indicated what kingdom they had come from, and if that wasn't enough, the creatures hauling them were dead giveaways.

Horses were native to only a small portion of the continent, so several kingdoms had to use other various beasts of burden. Many of them used creatures that could only be found within their borders, such as Sagima, who employed large rabbit-like creatures called Lago. Their massive feet made loud thumping sounds, unlike the beat of hoofs as the carriage approached.

A couple of carriages employed oxen, which are uncommon in Yulia. Celestine had only seen them a handful of times, but she never got over their dense muscular build compared to horses.

The five vehicles lined up in front of the trio, stopping with plenty of space between each other. Then, each driver stood, dismounting and taking their places in front of the carriage door. The one in front was the first to be opened, revealing a refined young woman who wore a large crown. She slowly descended the steps as the driver announced her arrival.

"Queen Emira of Minui has arrived," He called across the courtyard.

The other drivers let their passengers out as Queen Emira approached Celestine.

"Thank you for your hospitality, princess," She said, giving her a slight bow.

"It is nothing, Your Majesty. Thank you for your attendance," Celestine replied, returning the gesture.

Resuming an upright position, the queen, smiling, turned back toward her caravan who were all unpacking, including her own carriage driver. The castle staff on standby hurried to collect their things and assist in any way they could.

"The rest of my traveling party will greet you this evening, so please forgive their impropriety. After such a long trip, they're very tired," She apologized on behalf of the other royals.

The kingdom of Minui was the oldest and largest of the five nations that had formed the caravan. That, combined with their proximity, led to the formation of a coalition and Minui being dubbed the unofficial mother kingdom of the five. Whenever matters concerning the region came into question, Minui's opinion was viewed as more important than the others. Therefore, it was their queen who led the caravan.

"It is nothing. I look forward to seeing you all this evening," Celestine assured her.

The queen nodded, turning to check on her things. Celestine stayed behind long enough to ensure everyone was taken care of before heading to the ballroom.

She was pleased to find that everything was going smoothly there as well. Staff moved hurriedly around the room, putting the finishing touches on the decorations and setting out the tableware they would need to serve food later. Everything was in order just as she had ordered it to be, without so much as a hair out of place.

Surprisingly, she found Malachi standing off to the side, watching the staff work. He was leaning against a pillar, staring straight ahead with dead eyes. His expression seemed neutral, but the slightest bit of unease twisted the corners of his lips. He quickly shook that feeling off though, when he saw the three of them.

"Hello, you three. Everything going alright so far?" He asked, grinning and stepping away from the pillar.

"Yes, the first of the guests have arrived, so I came over to check on things here," Celestine replied.

She looked down, noticing the fine white suit Malachi wore. He was dressed to the nines, including a deep purple cape on top that covered his shoulders. It was far removed from his usual manner of dress like he had something to prove this evening. Which was odd considering he had a great deal to prove at the exhibition, but he didn't dress this fancy back then.

"Wonderful. Could you, uh… run the guest list by me again? I want to make sure it's fresh on my mind," He asked nervously.

Celestine nodded, quickly rattling off the names of each attending royal, as well as what kingdom they were from.

"And the rejections?"

She listed those as well, earning a perplexed look from him. He shifted on his heels, turning away to look back at the staff.

"Alright. I guess I'll see you again in a few hours.' He spoke without looking at her.

"See you later," Celestine replied, too busy to stay and try to analyze his demeanor.

The remaining hours leading up to the ball were a blur. Celestine and her entourage moved around the castle, checking on things and assisting where needed. When it was nearly time to begin, Auberon tapped on her shoulder and let her know. They then quickly headed to the ballroom entryway, where they intended to greet the guests as they were let in.

As they passed the windows overlooking the front entrance, Celestine paused and peeked outside. The sun started setting, and bathed everything in an orangish red hue. She looked down and was shocked to see the crowd that had formed. Countless nobles stood in front of the steps, chatting amongst themselves. Behind them, even more nobles were arriving in fancy carriages lined up past the castle gate. They stepped out with the help of their attendants, joining the others in front of the steps.

Some guests were coming in from kingdoms that were so far away that it would have taken months for them to arrive if they were to travel by carriage. They used magic to shorten the trip, either using teleportation arrays or fast-travel enchantments.

Amongst the crowd, Celestine could see some of these guests appearing out of thin air, their finely pressed clothes looking entirely unbothered by the trip. She was intimidated, but she buried those feelings quickly and continued toward the ballroom, knowing she had to prove herself today.

There was a short hallway that led from the ballroom entrance over to the main castle steps, allowing visitors to go directly into the ballroom if need be. That same hallway could also be used to access other parts of the castle, but today, all foot traffic would be directed into the ballroom. In this hallway, thirty feet inward from the main entrance, she planned to greet the guests before ushering them into the party. The trio took their places in the center of the hall but stopped when they realized their fourth member was missing.

"Malachi!" Celestine called out, hoping he was close enough to hear her.

She scanned the nearby area, finally noticing him standing by a window. He looked longingly down into the courtyard at all the carriages pulling in. At first, he didn't hear her, so she shouted a second time, making him finally turn.

"My apologies, princess," He called back as he quickly hurried to her side.

Once again, she could tell something was bothering him, but she didn't have time to acknowledge it. She watched the awkward way he fiddled with himself once he made it to her side. With him in place, she announced it was time to open the

Chapter 14

door.

Chapter 15

A swarm of nobility rushed into the hall as soon as the doors were opened. Not caring about introductions, they all walked toward the ballroom, chatting idly. When they reached Celestine and her group, they bowed politely and thanked her for the invitation before heading inside. For many of them, this was just an excuse to party

The first thirty guests or so all blended together. They were coming in so fast that Celestine couldn't keep them all straight. She greeted them as politely as she could but forgot their names seconds later as the next person walked up. Greeting them all was making her head spin.

From their place on the platform, they could hear the music and sounds of revelry coming from inside, and from what they could hear, everything was going great. It seemed to be off to a good start if only they could keep it that way.

The four planned to stand out front, greeting people for about 30 to 45 minutes, depending on the flow of attendees pouring in. They would head inside and join the fun once it was down to a slow trickle.

Now that the initial rush was gone, each group of nobles approached the platform, introduced themselves, and thanked Celestine profusely for her hospitality. She returned their sentiments and encouraged them to enjoy themselves at the party, gesturing for them to go ahead. Now that it was a slower pace, she could actually focus. It was prim and proper, very impersonal, but occasionally, one of them would break script.

"I must say, the performance at Viridisia's magic exhibition was incredible. I hope to see your skills again someday," A prince from a foreign country said, looking at Malachi.

Malachi bowed. "Thank you, Your Highness. I would love to perform for you again. Perhaps Princess Celestine and I could make a trip to visit you someday in the future?"

"Absolutely! We can make arrangements later," The prince replied with a massive grin before heading into the party.

Malachi's nervousness from earlier seemed to have disappeared, or he was just doing a good job distracting himself. Any time a member of nobility addressed him directly, he found a way to spin the conversation toward a future visit, opening doors for further diplomacy. It was perfect; he opened the doors, and Celestine looked more and more like a respectable leader.

She put extra care into her greetings toward members of the nobility who came from kingdoms that had been prosecuted by Yulia in the past. When the elf king and queen came, she made a point to bow deeply and thank them for their presence. She could see it on their faces when she straightened back up that her behavior had impressed them. No members of Yulian royalty had ever bowed to them in the past.

It had been centuries since any member of royalty coming

from a kingdom with magic had stepped foot in Yulia for fear of persecution. Even after the ban was lifted, many chose to stay away to protect themselves, just in case things hadn't improved as much as they claimed, but today, they got to see for themselves the steps the future queen was taking to make amends. Although far from perfect, Yulia was headed in the right direction, and the other kingdoms could respect that.

Everything was going perfectly until the stream of people coming in started to slow down, and Malachi's apprehension returned. He glanced around nervously again, scanning the crowd like a mouse watching for eagles. It wasn't like him, and it worried Celestine. She had the support of Vivian and Auberon, but Malachi was her mentor. Seeing the man she looked up to the most looking frazzled scared her.

There was no time to address it, however, so she went back to greeting guests, planning to check on him once they were in the ballroom. Off in the distance, she could see through the door as guests walked up the final few steps. As she watched for any remaining stragglers, the top of someone's head came into view. With a few more steps, she could tell it was a man with a head full of long black hair that he had pulled back under his crown. On the sides of his head, he had two large curled ram horns tucked back against his cheeks. He reached the landing, and she could finally see just how massive this man was. He had to be at least eight feet tall, with broad shoulders that made him look like a living wall. A well-decorated wall at that, he was dressed to the nines and draped with jewelry and bangles made of fine metals and precious stones. His attire was sharp in appearance, almost military-like, but still maintained the elegance and allure of a traditional royal attire.

Celestine quickly ran through the guest list in her mind to

try to remember who this could be, but she couldn't think of anything.

Beside the newcomer was another man with short goat-like horns who was only about 6 foot five. Compared to the first man, he looked tiny. His clothes were also nowhere near as extravagant, so Celestine assumed he was the attendant.

At the sight of them, Malachi made a tiny noise in his throat, an involuntary "eep" that made Celestine turn to him. His entire body was frozen, and he stared at the approaching guests in pure horror. She wanted to address him, but the duo made it up to the platform before she could, and the attendant stepped forward to make the introduction.

"Your Highness, I present to you King Aegis of Draconéa," He called out as he bowed.

Everyone on the platform bowed in return, except for Malachi, who stood stock still and looked down at him expectantly. Celestine wanted to get on to him, but there was no time. King Aegis gave them all an unenthusiastic once-over. His red eyes moved from one end to the other, never spending more than a few seconds on any given person. His gaze then returned to Celestine. His slit pupils barely seemed to register her.

"Thank you for your hospitality, Princess," He said flatly, walking away before she could reply, his attendant right behind.

Flustered by his impassiveness, Celestine didn't know what to say other than "um", and he was too far off to hear her say it anyway. She felt dumb, tapping her foot in frustration.

"It's alright, Princess. King Aegis has always been antisocial and rough around the edges, especially toward Yulian royalty. The fact that he showed up and greeted you is a huge success," Auberon reassured her, placing a hand on her shoulder.

She sighed, nodding to acknowledge what Auberon said, but it was then that she remembered Malachi's rude behavior, how he refused to bow, and turned to reprimand him when she found him standing there shaking. His face was stark white, and his eyes looked dead as he stared off into space.

"It's been long enough. Auberon, stay here and greet the final stragglers. Vivian, keep an eye out. I'll be back for you both in just a moment," Celestine delegated before dragging Malachi off to a secluded corner.

Call it nosey or observant. Either way, the princess made it a point to pay attention to the moods of those around her. It often came in handy when one was trying to read the room during diplomatic negotiations. The butting into people's business part was a side effect of her incessant desire to help people.

"What is wrong with you?" She asked him once she knew they were alone.

"H-He looked right through me. It was like I wasn't even there," Malachi spoke barely above a whisper.

"What?"

Malachi was still shaking, so she put her hands on his upper arms to steady him. He started to hyperventilate, leaning against the wall for support.

"Hey, hey, it's okay. I'm here. Whatever's wrong, you can talk to me," Celestine reassured him in a gentle whisper.

Malachi was silent for a moment before groaning and straightening back up.

"Alright. Let's see, um… where do I even start?" He began, rubbing the back of his neck. "He's my….. Ex."

"Ex what?"

"Ex-boyfriend," He elaborated.

Celestine blinked in confusion, processing. When it hit her, she gasped.

"You dated King Aegis?"

"Well, don't act too surprised," Malachi replied in a hurt tone.

"Sorry, it's just humans and draconéans don't mix. I wouldn't have expected that."

"I know. Even back in my day, they didn't."

"Why did you two break up?" She asked, trying to get to the root of the problem.

Simply being exes with someone wouldn't cause such a visceral reaction upon seeing them. His expression soured at the question.

"See, it's a long story, but to sum it up, I left him in a *very* cruel way."

"Really? What'd you do, leave him at the altar?"

"Worse. I won't get into specifics, but just know that I did something horrible, and I'm terrified to face him," Malachi explained.

Celestine was surprised to hear him admit to doing something like that, but the look in his eyes told her he was telling the truth. Even if she didn't want to believe he was capable of doing that, she had to accept it. The tinge of sadness in his expression gave her hope that maybe he had a reason.

"Well, you're going to have to face him sometime. Maybe you can ask for his forgiveness today? I'll be right there with you," Suggested Celestine.

Grimacing, he crossed his arms.

"Look, kiddo. This isn't something that can be fixed with an apology and a hug. It's more like the kind of thing you bury and hope it doesn't claw its way back out."

Celestine huffed. "Well, you won't know until you try. I tell you what, I order you to at least say hi to him and offer to dance."

"But I-"

"It is an order from your princess," Celestine shut him down.

Knowing he had to obey, Malachi rolled his eyes and shuffled his feet, desperately racking his brain for a way out of it.

"Fine, I'll ask him to dance, but that is it. Don't expect too much, though," He relented.

"Perfect. I'll be there if you need me, so let's do this!"

She took his hand and ran off back to Vivian and Auberon. All the attendees were already in the ballroom by then, so the main doors had been shut. They stood chatting, turning when they noticed Malachi and the princess approaching. After a quick check-in, the four of them headed inside and were greeted by an enthusiastic cheer from the crowd.

"There they are! The woman of the hour! The greatest magician in the world!" The people nearby praised them.

They bowed and mingled their way into the crowd. Auberon went off on his own to do some diplomatic schmoozing once he knew Celestine would be alright, while Vivian remained glued to Celestine's side. Malachi stayed with them momentarily before splitting off to chat on his own.

Knowing the drama brewing just beyond her sight made it hard for Celestine to focus on chatting. She promised she'd be there for him, but what if she was stuck in the middle of a conversation and couldn't? At the same time, though, she needed to make connections this evening.

Unlike at the exhibition, everyone was trying to impress her. They were practically tripping over themselves to get a chance to kiss her butt. They praised her behavior in Viridisia and told her how amazing her magician did. It was such an ego boost.

"Princess, this is such a wonderful party!" A princess who was only a few years older than her said as she approached.

"This is nothing. It is only thanks to wonderful guests like you."

"Thank you. How could I miss it? After the performance in Viridisia, I had to see more of the kingdom that produced such an amazing magician. Does he offer lessons?"

"So far, I am his only student, but he may be open to teaching more in the future," Celestine replied.

"Really? A Yulian princess with magic? That must be interesting," The Princess sipped her drink.

"It has been, but our kingdom has changed a lot since the ban was lifted. Hopefully, under my leadership, we can bring magic back to Yulia," Celestine gave her sales pitch.

"Oh, that sounds wonderful. Hey, we have some amazing state-sanctioned magic schools back home in Meridia, and a few of them have been thinking of opening pilot programs in other nations. I can talk to my father about maybe opening one here. Your magician could even teach there," The princess suggested.

Celestine mentally squealed with joy.

"That would be great. We can discuss more another day, perhaps over tea?"

"That sounds perfect. I'll get in touch with you later, Princess Celestine."

With that, the princess returned to the crowd.

"Did you hear that, Vivian? A magic school in Yulia! Think of the jobs that would create, oh! And the diplomacy!" She raved as she did a little dance to herself.

"Yes, Princess! That's wonderful. You are an excellent conversationalist," Vivian celebrated with her.

At that moment, the crowd around her had fizzled out, giving her a chance to reassess. She quickly scanned the crowd, checking to see where everyone was and how they were doing. Her parents had come in at some point, probably while she was busy talking, and were currently chatting with a small group of nobility they were already acquainted with. Toward the other side of the room, Auberon was busy telling a story to a group of enthralled nobles who hung on to his every word. The song that played was calm and relaxing, the perfect moment for her to make her speech.

"Follow me," She said to Vivian before dragging her over toward the band.

She whispered to one of the members, letting her know what was happening, then grabbed a glass of wine and a spoon. When the song ended, the band didn't start another one. In the resulting silence, Celestine began to tap her glass with her spoon to get everyone's attention.

"Hello everyone! I hope you're having a good time," She began as silence filled the room.

In the audience, she spotted Queen Hualing, who gave her a thumbs-up.

"I'm so happy to have such an amazing turnout this evening. As many of you know, one of my goals as the next leader of Yulia is to undo the years of damage my predecessors did to innocent members of the magic community. Their hatred and bigotry are a blight on our past, one that has kept us from meeting some amazing people and doing amazing things. I myself would have been a victim of their tirade, but thankfully, we have already come a long way. Today, with all of you as my witnesses, I vow to lead my kingdom to a future where those with magic live in harmony with those without. As long as I live, I will continue to serve this goal, and I thank you all for your kindness and understanding!"

She raised her glass to the audience and held her breath. If they raised their glasses now, it was a sign of solidarity, but if they refused, they were also refusing her message. She waited, nervously hoping for the best.

Starting at the front, people began to raise their glasses. It rippled across the ballroom until everyone had a glass in the air. Celestine relaxed, finally exhaling.

"Cheers!" She called out.

The audience repeated it and then drank their drinks. She did the same, happily gulping down several big sips. Vivian watched it all from her place over to the side. Tears threatened to slip from her eyes as she watched her princess bathe in the audience's cheers. She was so proud.

With her speech done, Celestine told the band they could continue, walking away as the next song played. Vivian fell into place behind her, following her as she snaked through the crowd.

"Incredible speech, Princess. I think they were moved by your fervor," Vivian praised, but her words fell on deaf ears: Celestine was busy looking for someone.

"I was thinking, Princess, perhaps we could relax a little. Maybe share a dan-" Vivian shyly proposed, but she stopped when she noticed how wildly Celestine was looking around.

Tabling her idea, she joined the search, looking around despite not knowing what they were searching for. She was just about to ask when Celestine honed in on her target.

Malachi was standing off to the side of the dance floor. He had his arms crossed and was hiding behind a pillar. She followed his gaze and saw that he was watching King Aegis, who was currently having a drink. He stared at the crowd from above his glass, his eyes showing indifference with a twinge of animosity.

People actively avoided him, meaning he was alone except for his attendant, who acknowledged the crowd with a similar grimace. This was a perfect opportunity for Malachi, but he hesitated.

Celestine moved through the crowd, greeting people as she went until she was in his line of sight. Seeing her pulled him from his silent staring.

"Go talk to him," She mouthed, gesturing at King Aegis.

"But the attendant," He mouthed back an excuse.

Celestine groaned.

"Come on! I'll find a way to distract him."

She looked around for Auberon, planning to use him, but King Aegis finished his drink as she did. Not seeing any waiters nearby, he asked his attendant, who happily agreed, to take the glass for him. Celestine turned back to Malachi with a smug grin as King Aegis was left alone.

Out of excuses, Malachi gulped before taking his first cautionary step. The space between the two men was crowded, allowing him to cross the room unnoticed.

Celestine followed from a distance, wanting to hear every bit of what was going to happen. She believed everything would go fine, that King Aegis would accept his dance, and that Malachi would see that he had nothing to worry about. In fact, she was excited for him to rekindle an old flame and wanted to see him happy.

The song that was playing as Malachi emerged from the crowd in front of Aegis was calm and slow, not romantic or exciting, just relaxing background music. A very neutral song to ask someone to dance to. Purple met red as the two men locked eyes.

"May I have this dance?" Malachi asked shakily as he extended his hand.

Celestine watched every movement carefully, noting how Malachi shook as King Aegis looked down at him. She watched as the king's ever-present indifference remained unchanged as he stared at the outstretched hand. Then she watched him turn and walk away.

Shocked, she moved to run over and stop him, but Malachi beat her to it, dashing in front of Aegis and extending his hand once again.

"May I have this dance?" He repeated, slower this time.

Again, Aegis looked down momentarily, then whipped around to leave. Malachi disappeared, then reappeared in front of him, hand still outstretched.

"May I have this dance?"

He had a determined look on his face, and finally, King Aegis's indifferent scowl fell. His face twisted into an expression of pure anger as he growled at Malachi. He stepped forward and shoved him away, walking past him as though he were dirt on the street. The shove nearly sent Malachi tumbling backward, but he kept his footing. He watched in silence as Aegis walked through the crowd, then up the stairs toward the outdoor balcony.

Anyone who was nearby stared at Malachi curiously. For many of them, this was their first time seeing the king of Draconéa, and he had just shoved a member of nobility from another kingdom. They were too scared to pry and instead whispered amongst each other.

"What happened?" Celestine asked as she ran up with Vivian, who was trailing behind her.

Malachi stood still, staring off in the direction Aegis had gone. His entire body was slouched over and limp like he was in shock, sweat beaded his forehead.

"I told you this wouldn't go well," He said, turning to Celestine.

She expected him to get mad at her over the outcome, but instead, he looked sad and disappointed.

"Wait, are you saying that's it?" She asked.

"Come on, you saw how he looked at me. It's probably best if we drop this whole thing and let everyone go back to their normal lives," He countered.

"Don't give me that. You can't just give up."

"Kiddo, this is it. I messed up, and now I'm dealing with the consequences. If I push anymore, I'll just end up hurting everyone involved."

There was pain in his voice as he spoke. It was a slight, tiny slip, but she could tell that he didn't mean what he was saying and longed to do more but feared the risks. She refused to let him run away, knowing that he would end up regretting it in the future.

"Go talk to him, try to apologize or something. I can't have my royal magician caught up in a feud with the king of a potential ally. You go up there right now, and I'll stay right behind you in case things get ugly," She commanded, leaving no room for argument.

He opened his mouth to fire back but shut it when he saw the look on her face. This was it; there was no worming his way out.

"Alright," He begrudgingly relented.

The two ladies followed him as he walked up the stairs and out towards the outdoor balcony. Despite its size and easy access from the ballroom, it was empty except for King Aegis, bent over the railing with his forehead resting against his arm. The

Chapter 15

sun had set a while ago, so the only light came from the open door to the ballroom. It was silent save for the noise coming from the party inside, and a slight evening breeze fluttered across. Slowly, Malachi began to approach.

Chapter 16

Celestine grabbed Vivian's hand as she watched Malachi, gripping it tight. She was so focused that she didn't notice how Vivian blushed and smiled.

Malachi slowly approached the balustrade, fiddling with his hands in front of his chest. Each step was slow and deliberate, making as little sound as possible. He was trying to come up with something to say but was drawing a blank.

"I'm sorry for bugging you earlier. I wa-" He tried to break the ice, but Aegis cut him off.

"Six hundred years. I waited over six *hundred* years without a word from you," He began without turning.

Malachi flinched, his entire body curling in on itself. "I was, um.."

Aegis whipped around, his face marred with rage.

"Then I hear a rumor about Yulia's new redheaded magician, some distant uncle with skills unlike anything seen before. I had to come to see for myself," He stepped away from the rail, walking predatory toward Malachi. "And what do I get? You didn't even have the nerve to speak or greet me. Then you made a half-assed attempt to smooth things over with a dance. How pathetic can you be?"

The king's voice echoed across the balcony and likely would have spilled into the ballroom had the music and chatter not drowned it out. Despite not knowing the context of the situation, Vivian was enthralled.

"I can't believe this. Do you have any idea what you put me through? When I saw you standing there, I wanted to destroy you just like you destroyed my heart, but the thought of hurting you hurt worse than bottling it up. Now, you want to apologize to make yourself feel better about what you did, but I'm not going to let that happen. Take your apology and shove it!"

Aegis shoved past him and headed back toward the party, leaving him standing there in shock. Celestine and Vivian hurriedly straightened up, making it look like they had just walked up and seen nothing.

He paused to speak to them. "Please excuse my behavior. Thank you again for your hospitality."

His voice was perfectly flat, completely removed from the shouting match he had just stepped away from. She was amazed that he could be so calm and collected after such an emotional moment. She could only manage a weak "no worries" before he stepped away. She watched him walk back into the party and head toward one of the staff members. With his height, she was able to follow him through the crowd as he followed the staff member out of the ballroom.

She turned back to Malachi, who stood frozen in place like a deer caught in headlights. He didn't budge as she and Vivian approached, as though he didn't even know they were there. Unsure what to say, Celestine placed a hand on his shoulder.

"Well, that could have gone worse," Malachi laughed, but it was a broken laugh, on the verge of tears.

"Are you alright?"

"I'm still alive, which is good. I was half expecting him to toss me off the side of the balcony." He turned to her with a grin, but when he saw the serious look on her face, he stopped. "I um... I'm sorry for bringing my drama to your big night."

Celestine sighed.

"It's alright. This altercation was going to happen eventually, and I think the ball helped King Aegis quell his rage a little for fear of causing a greater scene than he did. We can discuss this again later, but Malachi, I want you to know that I can't help you unless I know all the details."

"I'm not ready to talk about it yet," He looked off into the crowd. "I'm going to turn in for the night, and we can talk about it another day."

"Alright," She relented.

Princess Celestine didn't want to let him go, but she could see how exhausted he looked and knew that pushing the subject wouldn't solve anything. Even if he told her everything right then and there, King Aegis had already left. It was an unfortunate predicament.

After a quick exchange of "good night's" Malachi left, sneaking through the crowd to head back to his room, and the two ladies returned to the party feeling confused and conflicted. They tried not to let it show on their faces, but everything they had witnessed was complicated and depressing. Her brother Hesperus was the first to notice, quickly swimming through the crowd to check on her.

"Hey, is everything alright?" He asked.

He was dressed in his finest princely wear, with the sword of

Yulia attached to his hip. Not much of a party person, he had spent most of the night wandering around to kill time. He was only there for appearance's sake, so he was planning to leave soon, but when he saw his sister's expression, he changed his mind.

"Yeah. Just had some personal stuff come up."

"On your part or someone else's?"

"Someone else's. I'm alright," She clarified, noticing a rather tall person sneaking through the crowd toward them.

"Pardon me, Princess Celestine, Prince Hesperus," King Aegis's attendant apologized once he broke through. "But have you seen King Aegis? We separated earlier, and I haven't been able to find him since."

Hesperus turned to address the newcomer but froze in place once they made eye contact. His eyes went wide, and his jaw went slack. The attendant looked him up and down, confused by his reaction.

"He wen-" Celestine began, but Hesperus cut her off.

"I'm sure one of the attendants saw where he went. Here, we can go look for him together."

He gestured for him to follow, then led the attendant off. The ladies let them go, curious about Hesperus's behavior. They made a mental note to ask him about it later.

By then, the party was in its final hour, and the crowd was slowly losing its energy. Her parents had already turned in for the night, the band was playing slow songs, and the hors d'oeuvres were running low. Celestine was mentally drained but had an impression to maintain, so she returned to the crowd. After a while of aimless wandering, she found Auberon, who quickly took his place by her side.

With all the excitement of the evening, she was able to ignore her anxiety and get through it without him. It would have been nice to share a dance.

"Have you had a fruitful evening, Princess?" He asked.

"I think so. What about you?"

Auberon pulled out a notebook. "I spoke with the nobility from a total of twenty-two different nations, ten of which were current allies. Of the remaining twelve, eight agreed to meet for tea at a later date, and the other four invited you to upcoming events at their kingdoms. While we spoke, I brought up some potential benefits of collaborating but made no promises."

He spent the next few minutes further detailing his conversations and the topics discussed. From the sound of it, he did a better job selling Yulia than she did, just as she expected from him. He was so well organized and confident, she was blown away, and it made her feel self-conscious about her own performance.

"Would you like me to send letters next week on your behalf to the non-allied countries in attendance?" He concluded.

"That sounds perfect. We can meet the day after tomorrow to discuss what to include in the letters. Will you be available for tomorrow's send-off?"

She planned to have a big goodbye party for all the attendants tomorrow, including breakfast served in the outer courtyard. Then she and whichever employees were available, preferably Vivian and Auberon, would personally send them off.

"I should be unless something comes up."

"Perfect, and Vivian, how about you?"

"I will be wherever you need me to be, princess," She replied.

"Great."

Celestine looked around the room, checking out of the

conversation to monitor the few remaining guests. She looked for anyone who looked bored or uncomfortable, then swooped in to talk them out of it. If she couldn't cheer them up, Vivian or Auberon figured out a way.

The trio stuck together for the remainder of the night. Even as fatigue settled in, they continued to smile and greet guests or dance if someone asked. They brought out food and drink when needed, even serving it to people like proper hosts. The guests were shocked by Celestine's willingness to humble herself.

There were several nobles among the crowd who came from kingdoms that were previously discriminated against by Yulia. Everyone watched in amazement as Celestine poured glasses of wine for them. She served drinks to people who weren't human, who were members of the groups that Yulian royalty had tried to massacre in the past like it was nothing. For many, it was impressive, a sign that Celestine planned to take the kingdom in a new direction, but for some, they saw it as Yulia losing their way. After her speech earlier, people scrutinized her behavior more than they would have otherwise.

It was nearly midnight when the final guests decided to call it quits. The entire staff breathed a sigh of relief, had a quick celebration for making it through, and then got to work cleaning up. Celestine stayed momentarily to assist the servants as a thanks for all their hard work before heading to bed, her feet dragging like two cinder blocks.

It took all the strength she had to get up the next morning. Every atom in her body was tired, and she felt impossibly stiff. Obligations be damned, she couldn't do it...... With a loud groan, she forced herself up and climbed out of bed.

Breakfast was in full swing when she made it down to

the front. The attendants ran around delivering platters of breakfast food to hungry patrons sitting at tables in the courtyard and keeping the buffet line fully stocked. Everything smelled incredible. Her mouth was watering as soon as she caught a whiff of it all. As she passed by the first table, she grabbed a pastry and then headed into the crowd to mingle. Most people were either tired or hungover from the night before, so she knew they wouldn't have enough energy to get rowdy.

She moved from group to group like a social butterfly collecting nectar, forcing herself to talk to people to distract herself from her anxiety. Several people praised her party and her hospitality, to which she humbly declined their praise.

Vivian and Auberon joined the party around noon. After greeting Celestine, they started mingling with the crowd, doing their best to represent their nation properly. Auberon quickly found his place among a group of dignitaries who were in the middle of discussing the barley trade in the West. Celestine caught a little of it as she walked by and was amazed by how sophisticated Auberon sounded as he provided his own insight.

Once again, he made her feel stupid. She's the princess, and one day, she's going to be queen. She's supposed to be the one who knows everything. What kind of queen would she be if she had to rely on him for knowledge forever? Spiraling into the abyss of self-deprecation, she walked through the crowd like nothing was wrong. She was so deep in her feelings that she didn't even notice someone stepping in front of her until she bumped into them.

"Oh my goodness, I'm so sorry!" She apologized profusely.

"It's alright."

Looking up, Celestine realized it was Malachi that she had

run into. He smiled down at her, but he was looking worse for wear. There were deep bags under his eyes, and the skin on his cheeks was red and irritated. If she had to guess, she'd say he was probably up all night crying.

"I was thinking we could start training back up after tomorrow. That way, you have enough time to recuperate after all this," He suggested, breaking the silence.

"Yes! That sounds good. I'm going to have a lot to do after everyone leaves," Celestine fumbled a response.

Malachi nodded sheepishly.

"I'm gonna go get some breakfast. Have fun, kiddo," He said before heading into the crowd.

Celestine went back to her mingling once he left. She kept an eye out for King Aegis or his assistant the entire time. She wanted to apologize for everything that had gone on the day before and potentially open up a dialogue about a solution to their problems, but no matter how hard she looked, she couldn't find them.

On the way around, a couple of members of royalty stopped her, including a princess close to her age who had an assistant carrying her bags with her. Celestine recognized her as the princess of the semiaquatic people of Anduma: Princess Angela.

"Thanks for everything, Princess Celestine," Angela said, the gills on her neck flexing with each word.

Up until Yulia legalized magic, the people of Aduma were not allowed. Then, it took several years of diplomacy for them to even consider stepping foot within the kingdom, so Celestine was one of the first members of Yulian royalty to speak with an Aduman princess. She did her best not to stare at her flexing gills.

"You're so welcome, Princess Angela. I apologize for not

having enough time for a dedicated conversation with you," She replied, picking each word carefully.

Princess Angela smiled.

"Don't worry about it. I've got to leave now, but maybe this summer, when the waters have warmed up, I could take you for a ride on some of my family's hippocampi. They're the fastest in my kingdom."

"That sounds lovely. I look forward to it."

Princess Angela waved goodbye, then walked with her assistant toward her carriage. There were several other carriages lined up by the stairs as nobles slowly started to leave. Following Angela, she checked the line, looking for the Draconéan crest, but it was nowhere to be found. Frustrated, she once again went back to socializing. A few minutes later, she ran into her brother, who was always scanning the crowd.

"Good morning, Princess," He greeted when he saw her.

"Good morning, Prince. How did everything go last night with the assistant? Did you get him squared away?"

Hesperus's face flushed at the mention of the assistant, and he rubbed the back of his neck shyly.

"Yeah. He and I actually talked for a while. His name's Jasper."

"Oh really? I'm glad to hear that."

Hesperus smiled before going on.

"We got to talking about sparring, and I tried to talk him into sparring one day, but he didn't give me a definitive answer."

Suddenly, an idea hit Celestine, and her eyes lit up.

"Hey! This is perfect!"

"It is?" Hesperus questioned.

"Yes! Malachi and King Aegis aren't getting along, don't ask, but if you and Jasper become friends, then we could use your friendship to break the ice," She explained.

"You want to exploit my friendship?"

"Exploit is a nasty word, but yes," Celestine sighed. "Look, allyship with Draconéa would be so good for Yulia economically, but more than that, I want to help Malachi out. Do you think you could help me on this one?"

Hesperus looked away with a frustrated look on his face.

"Fine, but promise you won't interfere with me and Jasper."

"Absolutely! Now, can you help me find them? We need to give them a proper send-off."

Celestine took her brother's hand and led him around. They walked back and forth from the line of carriages to the tables where people were socializing. Each time, they kept an eye out for King Aegis or Jasper. Since the two of them were so tall, they should have been easy to spot, but no dice. They were ready to give up when they saw a pair of horns sticking out above the crowd.

"There!" Celestine pointed.

The two kept their eyes trained on the horns until King Aegis and Jasper stepped out of the dense crowd, allowing them to see more than just their horns. The two were dressed more casually than the night before, with King Aegis wearing pants and a suit jacket, while Jasper had an entire butler getup. Celestine looked to the side and saw their carriage pulling up, so it was now or never.

"Come on," She said, grabbing her brother and pulling him along.

As quick as she could, she waded through the crowd toward them. As she got closer, she was able to see their faces better and tell what they were doing. Jasper walked about two steps behind King Aegis and pulled their bags behind him. He had a paper in his free hand and was reading from it. Meanwhile,

King Aegis walked with his shoulders squared and a frustrated look. There were bags under his eyes like he didn't get enough sleep.

Celestine tried to hurry, but the two of them reached their carriage before she could reach them. She panicked, watching as Aegis helped Jasper put the bags on the luggage rack. There was only one way she could think of to stall them.

"King Aegis!" She yelled as she rushed through the remaining fifteen feet between them.

He didn't hear her the first time, so she yelled even louder, throwing up the hand that wasn't holding her brother's to get his attention. That time, it worked, and King Aegis turned back toward her. His expression softened slightly, going from annoyed to indifferent.

"I hope you slept well last night. Sorry again for everything that happened. I was hoping we could-"

She was so close to him when, suddenly, an explosion nearly flipped King Aegis's carriage. Debris went flying in all directions, hitting anyone and anything nearby. The more alert nobles and attendants were able to raise their shields in time or use protective magic, but the others didn't escape getting hit.

A cloud of smoke covered where the carriage, King Aegis, and Jasper had been, making it impossible to see anything. Celestine had thrown her arms up to protect herself, but she panicked as soon as things settled down.

"King Aegis! Jasper!" She yelled, scared they may have been injured.

Hesperus let go of her hand and rushed forward, hand on his sword, ready to go. He looked around feverishly, trying to catch sight of the missing nobility or the attackers. When the dust settled, they found King Aegis standing there, looking entirely unbothered. The only sign he had just been next to an explosion was the dust on his shoulder, which he brushed off. Jasper was off to the side and had his arms outstretched in front of him. He had put up a protective barrier for himself, knowing King Aegis wouldn't be harmed, sparing him from injury.

Their carriage was another story, though. The explosion tore the left side apart, sending wood splinters a good thirty feet in every direction. The wheels on that side were gone, and massive cracks ran through the remaining body structure. Celestine and Hesperus were only spared because King Aegis and Jasper inadvertently shielded them.

Turning back to the crowd, Celestine saw that several guests had been injured by flying debris. The explosion rocked the entire courtyard, and the shock wave impacted many who weren't hit by debris. Injured nobles lay on the ground, moaning in pain, as their traveling companions scrambled to help them. Vivian and Auberon came running, relieved when they saw Princess Celestine unharmed, but their relief was short-lived since they still didn't know who had done this.

"Everyone, tend to the injured," Celestine ordered.

Staff members and anyone willing to help hurried to help anyone they could see. They helped them stand or got to work tending their wounds. Hesperus and Celestine went to King Aegis, with Hesperus on high alert. He unsheathed the enchanted sword and kept it in his hands, not taking any chances.

"Are you alright?"

"I'm fine. Tell me, Princess, is this how your parties normally end?" Aegis replied, a hint of malice in his voice.

Behind them, Malachi burst through the crowd, out of breath. He came running as soon as he saw what happened. He relaxed when he saw Aegis was uninjured.

"No, never. I don't know what that was," Celestine reassured him.

Aegis went to respond, but a loud voice cut through the chaos out in the courtyard.

"Attention!" Someone yelled.

Everyone turned, and a group of about ten people appeared before them. They appeared out of thin air, materializing where everyone could see them. They all wore similar full-body suits of armor with a strange symbol on their chests. It looked like an image of a sun with rays of light shooting out and killing a creature at the bottom that looked like a mix between a dragon and a demon. At the head was a female whose face was covered by a helmet. She had a spear in her hand and aggressively tapped it on the ground.

"For too long, the royalty of Yulia has allowed magic to desecrate its once sacred grounds," The woman began, loud enough for everyone there to hear. "The one bright beacon of hope has grown dim under their rule. They have allowed monsters in their midst, monsters they once fought valiantly. That is why today, we, the Old Guard, have decided to make a stand. We denounce the current state of Yulia and demand you return to the proper ways of old!"

Celestine was frozen in shock. Their words were confusing and terrifying. It was a direct threat against her and her people, and she wasn't equipped to handle it.

Chapter 17

A loud yell finally pulled Celestine out of it. Vivian rushed up beside her, positioning herself between the attackers and Celestine and pushing past Prince Hesperus. She held her sword in front of her, poised to strike.

"Anyone who dares to threaten the Yulian royal family will have to answer to me!" She proudly declared.

The "Old Guard," as they called themselves, turned to her: one lonely soldier risking everything for her princess. They laughed, taunting her.

"One pathetic knight, only one of you is foolish enough to defend Yulia?" The leader goaded the audience.

Vivian growled, adjusting her footing. Behind her, a few more guards recovered and came to help. They lined up around Celestine. Hesperus joined her as well, standing by her side in a similar stance.

King Aegis and Jasper watched curiously, not wanting to get involved.

"Your attempts will be met with-" The leader attempted to

launch into another speech but was cut off when a small orb exploded beside her head.

Like a smoke bomb, a cloud of brightly colored smoke filled the area. Several more bombs came one after another, filling the entire courtyard with colorful smoke. The Old Guard gasped and coughed, getting the stuff in their lungs while the guests backed away to spare themselves.

Malachi came running up with two more of the bombs ready in his hands. He stopped in front of King Aegis to reassess. He closed his fists, and the orbs disappeared. Then he raised his right arm and snapped his fingers. Instantly, the cloud of smoke ignited and burned away, leaving the courtyard empty.

Everyone was shocked silly, frozen in place, but Celestine forced herself out of it, knowing that she needed to be a leader at that moment. She ran over to Malachi.

"Did you kill them?" She asked, looking at the empty place where they had just been standing.

"No, that fire wasn't hot enough to kill, and even if it were, their armor would have been left," Malachi explained.

He turned to King Aegis with a worried look. Their eyes met momentarily, and Malachi smiled, but Aegis turned away coldly.

With the threat gone, Vivian rushed over to Celestine. Hesperus remained with the other guards, looking to see where the attackers went.

"Your Highness! Are you okay? Did anything hit you?" She asked, carefully checking her over.

From behind her, Auberon ran over, concern written all over his face. Hearing him coming, Vivian became acutely aware of her hands resting on Celestine's shoulders, and she pulled them back, blushing.

Chapter 17

"Celestine! Were you hurt?" Auberon asked as he tried to catch his breath.

"No, I'm fine. Help me take stock of the injured. Vivian, work with the other guards to see if you can find any sign of where those creeps left or came from," She ordered.

Vivian snapped up, nodded, and then took off to perform her duties. Auberon went to check on the injured, and just as Celestine went to follow him, someone grabbed her arm and stopped her. It was one of the guest kingdom's nobles. He looked angry and confused, as if he needed someone to yell at, and she was the only one nearby.

"What was *that*?! A piece of debris hit my wife, she could have been killed!" He yelled, demanding an explanation. '

All the confidence inside Celestine was instantly zapped from her system. She tried to string together an apology, anything to placate him, but he shut her down.

"Why weren't we informed that Yulia has terrorists? Do you not care about your guests?"

His ranting and raving drew the attention of nearby guests, and they turned to see what the fuss was about. Malachi was still nearby, and when he heard the commotion, he hurried over to defend her, but King Aegis went ahead of him. He grabbed the crazed guest and pulled him away from Celestine, silencing his rant. The man went pale at the sight of the king. His arm looked like a twig when held in Aegis's grasp.

"Today's attack was not Yulia's fault. It was aimed at the entire magic community, and Yulia was used to make a statement. They are victims just like us," He stated.

Since he was the one most affected by the attack, his words on the matter carried more weight. He pulled his arm from Aegis's grasp and left to check on his wife. Malachi breathed a sigh of relief now that Celestine wasn't being harassed. Behind them, they could hear Mr. Babic's shrill voice as he stepped out to see what had happened. He quickly got to work helping the nobles and ordering people around so Celestine could focus on figuring out what just happened.

Aegis turned to her now that the man was gone.

"Princess, we need to discuss what just happened. I don't believe it is safe for the remaining royals within the magic community to leave. They could be ambushed on their way. Is your castle equipped to care for them?" He asked.

"Yes... Yes! We have enough supplies for another two nights or so, but after that, I'll have to send for more," She replied, intimidated.

"Good. I'll help corral the gathered nobility. Will the ballroom work as a meeting place for now?"

"Yes. That would be perfect, actually."

King Aegis nodded. "I will work on that. Check with your staff out here, then head inside."

With that, the king walked away, calling out to the nobles to head inside and to the ballroom. She watched him point to direct people and even help up an injured guest. Then, she realized something: he was trying to help her out. King Aegis, the most infamous Yulia hater, was trying to help the Yulian princess. For a moment, she was shocked, but her shock was soon interrupted.

"Come on, Princess, we need to check on the staff like he said," Malachi put a hand on her shoulder.

"Ri- Wait, you were listening?"

"Yup. Heard every word," Malachi replied.

"From a distance?" Celestine asked, picturing him hiding as he listened.

"Yes. For strategic reasons," He lied.

Celestine laughed. "Alright, let's do this."

In total, there were 16 injured nobles and 8 injured staff. Thankfully, none of the injuries were major, and after a few days of medical care and some undisturbed rest, they would be fine. Celestine reassured each one personally before they were carried off to the castle's infirmary. She told them she wouldn't rest until the perpetrators were found and that her kingdom would happily care for them until they were healed. Some were frightened, but her kind words helped them settle down.

Normally, this was beyond the duties of a princess, but because these people had been injured in *her* kingdom after attending a party, which was *her* idea, she knew she needed to go above and beyond to make an impression.

Thanks to King Aegis's suggestion and the work of Vivian and Auberon, the crowd was directed into the ballroom, and the outer courtyard was secured in less than a half hour. They treated the area where the group had appeared as a crime scene, quartering it off to be inspected whenever resources became available.

She and Malachi headed inside once Celestine was certain the castle staff understood their orders. They went straight to the ballroom and were mobbed with questions as soon as they entered.

Celestine's parents had made it downstairs and were near the door when they walked in, so they were the first to ask questions.

"There you are, sweetie. Are you alright? Is everything okay?" Her mother asked, reaching out to check her over.

Before she could respond, nearby nobles started shouting

their questions.

"How could Yulia allow a terrorist attack?"

"Were your borders not secure enough?"

"Have the terrorists been caught yet?"

They were all talking over each other, too impatient and scared to take turns. They started closing in on her, getting closer and closer as they continued to hurl accusations her way. She was starting to suffocate; the crowd surging in on her felt like they were trying to squish her, and she started to panic.

"Everyone back away! We won't get anything done by randomly yelling questions all at once!" Malachi yelled, pushing his way in front of Celestine and her mother.

The nobles backed away, seeing the logic of his statement.

"Thank you. Now let's do this the right way," Malachi continued, turning to Celestine so she could take the floor.

Her mother moved aside, letting her daughter go. She stepped forward with a deep breath and a quick glance at her parents for reassurance.

"Everyone, today we were attacked by a terrorist group that was previously unknown to me and my kingdom. We aren't sure yet how they managed to get in or where they came from, but most of you heard them state their intentions," She began, doing her best to sound professional despite her fear. "I would like to formally denounce them here and now. The kingdom of Yulia regrets its past prejudices, and we will not allow this group of terrorists to intimidate us into regressing back to our old ways. Now, if any of you have any information on the matter, please speak up."

The crowd hung on to her every word. It wasn't the quick-fix solution they hoped for, but it reassured most of them that they weren't the victims of a backstabbing kingdom and that the ball wasn't a trap. They still had doubts, but for now, they had to work with Yulia to get answers.

Silence filled the ballroom until a man with cat ears, a Felidæde, stepped forward.

"There have been a series of small-scale attacks on some of my kingdom's supply routes lately. We assumed it was a group of bandits, nothing too significant, but we did get reports that the bandits bore regalia with a sun symbol," He offered up.

A second noble, a normal human man, raised his hand.

"We've had similar issues in Birria. We, too, assumed it was a group of bandits and didn't take it seriously. "

More nobles came forward with similar stories. From what they were saying, Celestine gathered that this group had been robbing supply caravans of various countries for the last few months. There didn't seem to be a pattern to the robberies: some were against countries with magic, but there were just as many against non-magic countries.

As the conversation began to slow down, King Aegis came forward. Everyone hushed when they saw he had something to say, and they all looked at him expectantly.

"About five years ago, there was an assassination attempt against me. The assailant managed to sneak into my throne room but was killed soon after. We found a tunic bearing that sun symbol on his person and a collection of maps with marked locations."

The crowd gasped.

"At the time, we were unsure what the maps meant since the marked areas didn't appear to have a pattern or explanation, so there was no telling what they meant. We waited to hear more, but nothing came of it. Even when I sent out a fleet of men to investigate the matter, they came up empty-handed. Still, I believe this organization has probably been acting for longer than we think, possibly over a decade." He finished.

The crowd began to mutter nervously once more, but Celestine stopped them.

"This is all great information, but for the time being, I don't believe there is much we can do. Besides, after all that excitement, I'm sure many of you are tired or worried about your injured loved ones. I don't believe it is wise to travel with these people still at large, so I suggest you all stay here for another night or so. Please return to the rooms you stayed at last night. I will have the staff care for you until you feel safe enough to leave. If you must travel, please do so in groups. Tomorrow, I request that all nobles from magic-affiliated countries meet with me to discuss our plans going forward. I will gladly meet with non-magic kingdoms, but since the terrorists are targeting magics, they will be the priority," She gave them all clear instructions.

With things decided, the crowd slowly dwindled as people left for the infirmary or their rooms. A few walked over and thanked Celestine for her hospitality and care, bowing as they did so. It made her feel so noble she could hardly stop herself from blushing.

Her parents gushed about how well she did once she was free, but then they, too, left. The King, unfortunately, had other matters that he couldn't wait to handle, but their daughter had a plan and was handling things well, so he knew it would be alright. He planned to attend the meeting tomorrow and get caught up on the situation.

Malachi stayed by her side the entire time, watching out for any other unruly nobles who might try to pin the blame on her. If one looked particularly rude, he gave them the nastiest glare he could manage. Any time Celestine looked his way, he gave her an encouraging smile.

The ballroom was nearly empty when King Aegis walked over to the two of them. Malachi went rigid as a board, but Aegis didn't even look at him. His gaze was focused entirely on Celestine.

"Princess, there is a matter I need to discuss with you regarding the assassin," He said, his voice grave.

"Absolutely, Your Majesty," She replied.

Aegis looked around.

"Not here, follow me," He said, turning and walking away.

Celestine and Malachi shared a glance.

"Should I come with you?" He asked, voice shaky.

"Yes, I could use the backup," She replied.

In reality, she didn't want to let him chicken out, but she couldn't say that. Malachi nodded, and the two followed King Aegis. He led them down the hall and around a few turns before he stopped. He checked to ensure no one was nearby before returning to the two of them. Again, he looked beyond Malachi like he was as insignificant as the stain on the wall beside his head and focused entirely on Celestine.

"I didn't want to say it in front of the others because I didn't want to start an uproar, but we found a series of documents on the assassin," He began.

"Documents?" Celestine asked.

"Yes, there were several that seemed like ordinary record keeping and planning: things the assassin would need to know to complete his mission, but others that appeared more sinister," He paused. "There were hand-drawn maps of Yulia's castle with newer sections added on afterward in a different color and notes along the outer edges that I couldn't understand. Various drawings of objects were also done in great detail, but they lacked descriptions. Instead, they had instructions on how to find them."

Malachi spoke up, the gears in his head turning a mile a minute. "The maps. Whoever drew the initial map could have been doing it from memory or from a map they stole, and then someone else could have added to it to bring it up to date. Is there any way we could cross-reference our maps to see which period the initial map came from?"

"The initial map was in line with the castle during the reign of King Nicodemus the First. I was familiar with the castle back then," King Aegis replied quickly, not even looking at Malachi.

Although the words themselves were casual, it felt like there was a change in the air. Malachi shifted in place like the subtext behind his words cut him like a knife.

"So either the person who drew the map was familiar with the castle during that time, or they copied a stolen map from that period," Celestine explained through the tension.

"Correct, and it would appear the assassin's next mission was to steal items from Yulia. When it happened, we didn't want to alarm you all if it wasn't necessary. After investigating, we couldn't find any evidence that he wasn't working alone, and since the assassin was dead, we believed everything was fine," Aegis added.

"And if they managed to steal something in the meantime?" Celestine questioned.

"Then we would have a lead on the culprit. With the initial agent dead, we believed whoever was behind it would either have to wait to find another or would back out and lie low for a while. It seems the latter came to fruition."

King Aegis paused, choosing his next words carefully.

"Princess, I'm afraid these people intend to start a new war against magic, and they plan to make Yulia the epicenter. Because my carriage was targeted today, I suspect they wish to target my kingdom first since our kind are some of the strongest magic users. Taking us down would cripple the community. In light of this, it would be wise for our kingdoms to team up."

Malachi perked up at the sound of that.

"Team up?" Celestine asked.

"Yes. By sharing intelligence, we could find the base of this group quicker than if we worked separately. We don't know how powerful they are yet, so combining our might would also be advantageous." '

King Aegis spoke calmly, plainly detailing the benefits of his plan. Having someone so experienced helping her made Celestine calm down. She felt like, as long as she had King Aegis and Malachi backing her, then those terrorists didn't stand a chance.

"I agree. We can work the fine details out later, but for now, we just need to rest and perform as much recon as possible. At tomorrow's meeting, we'll get everything we can out of the others," She said.

The king nodded.

"Good. I will see you tomorrow then," He said, turning to leave.

"W-were you hurt?" Malachi blurted out, stepping forward.

Celestine and King Aegis froze, not expecting him to speak. Aegis was turned away, so they couldn't see his expression, but they could almost feel the scowl he surely wore.

"What kind of stupid question is that? Of course not," He replied quickly, then left, not giving him a chance to continue.

Malachi deflated.

221

"Shouldn't have said that," He muttered.

"It was worth a shot," Celestine consoled.

He shook off the shame and turned back to her.

"Moving on, we should check in with the knights, maybe they've found something by now."

"Good idea," Celestine said, leading the way.

Unfortunately, the knights had nothing to report. Vivian's head was low as she detailed all the work they put into figuring things out, only to come up empty-handed. The intruders left nothing but marks on the ground where they stood. There were no carriage tracks, no footsteps, nothing they could follow. Not even a full forensic evaluation could turn up any leads. By all means, they had appeared out of thin air.

Celestine thanked her and the other knights regardless, and then she and Malachi moved on to check on the injured again. Auberon was there talking to everyone and ensuring they were well cared for. When he saw the princess, he gave a quick progress report, which was all good news regarding the recovery of the nobles.

"Thank you for all of your hard work," Celestine thanked him.

"For you, Princess, there is nothing I can't do," He replied, bowing deeply to her.

The sun was beginning to go down when Celestine and Malachi left the infirmary. They were exhausted and ready to head off to bed, but Malachi had one last thing to say.

"Princess, I can't help but think this is partially my fault."

"Why do you say that?" Celestine turned.

"Well, they showed up here in Yulia right after me, and I was the one pushing you to do a lot of this stuff," He replied, awkwardly rubbing the back of his neck.

"Nonsense. The way I see it, they were bound to attack. They just chose today because I was having a big party, that's all."

Malachi's face turned serious.

"But what if it's not? There have never been two magic users in the Yulian government at the same time before, and I can't get over that map. I mean, what are the chances that they chose a map from *my* father's reign?"

"Probably better than you think. I wouldn't worry too much. This is just a group of old-fashioned jerks that we have to squash, nothing more, nothing less," She reassured him and herself simultaneously.

His face softened.

"Alright, but if it comes down to it, I would rather leave and go back into exile than see you hurt, okay?" He said.

"Same to you, now go to bed. We need to be ready for the morning," Celestine laughed.

"Okay, goodnight," Malachi waved, then headed to his room.

Now that she was alone, Celestine's nerves flared up, nearly knocking her off her feet. She had to lean against the wall until she calmed down. This was all so much. Could she really protect her kingdom? Her head was already spinning just imagining the meeting in the morning. None of the years she spent studying and prepping could have prepared her for this.

She knew stressing about it this early wouldn't do her any good, so she forced herself to go to bed. Tomorrow's meeting was going to decide her next move. Until then, she could only hope her worst fears hadn't come true.

Made in the USA
Columbia, SC
10 September 2024

41553914R00126